LAUGH, CRY AND GLOW AS YOU READ
OF EVERYDAY EPISODES THAT SEEMED
TOUCHED BY THE HAND OF GOD

* The time Thyra mysteriously received "money from heaven" during a family crisis.

* A hazardous auto accident that would have proven fatal, save for the spiritual intercession of a friend's prayer.

* The worst midwestern snowstorm of the century that crippled everyone except Thyra, who found safe passage through the guidance of Mama's Way.

These and many other "common" miracles are guaranteed to flood your life with happy inspiration as they spill into your heart from the pages of each delightful chapter.

MAMA'S WAY
Thyra Ferré Bjorn

1980

Birthday from Sharon

This low-priced Bantam Book
has been completely reset in a type face
designed for easy reading, and was printed
from new plates. It contains the complete
text of the original hard-cover edition.
NOT ONE WORD HAS BEEN OMITTED.

RL 4, IL 7-up

MAMA'S WAY

A Bantam Book / published by arrangement with
Holt, Rinehart and Winston, a Division of CBS Inc.

PRINTING HISTORY

Holt, Rinehart and Winston edition published September 1959
8 printings by December 1972

The Christian Herald Family Book Shelf edition
published October 1959

Bantam edition / December 1976
2nd printing ...... September 1978
3rd printing .... January 1980

ISBN 0–553–13791–3

Published simultaneously in the United States and Canada

Bantam Books are published by Bantam Books, Inc. Its trade-
mark, consisting of the words "Bantam Books" and the por-
trayal of a bantam, is Registered in U.S. Patent and Trademark
Office and in other countries. Marca Registrada. Bantam
Books, Inc., 666 Fifth Avenue, New York, New York 10019.

PRINTED IN THE UNITED STATES OF AMERICA

To "Papa"
(Reverend Frans Ferré)
In loving memory this book is
dedicated

Chapter One

"**I** wish you would write a book about what you have told us here tonight," a minister said to me some months ago when, as a guest in their lovely home, I was about to bid him and his wife good night and retire.

"Yes, you really should," chimed in his charming young wife. "I wish we could have shared this evening with the whole world."

I was a bit perplexed as I looked at them.

"You mean a book mixing all the things we have talked about since we began at ten thirty P.M.? It would be a very religious book. I can't write books like that. My brother is the theologian. I stick to the home-spun family stuff."

The minister put his hand on my shoulder. "You might think I am fooling," he said, "but I am dead serious. And I don't mean you should write a book dealing with theology. I want you to write a book just the way you talk! Believe me, a book like that is very much needed in the world today. I have to confess I don't go all the way with you in your philosophy of life, but your talk has helped me. It has made me stop to think. We ministers so often get into a rut."

When I went to my room, his words kept echoing in my tired mind. This was the second time I had been invited to talk in his big church, and the second

1

time I had been a house guest at the parsonage. I loved coming here. They were a delightful young couple with wonderful youngsters. He was a promising minister who, I predicted, would go far in his calling, with just the right kind of wife to be a good helpmate during those busy long years ahead. And there was a certain hominess and warmth in this parsonage, and a welcome not just in words, but in the spirit that prevailed here. How well I understood why they were so loved and cherished by their congregation!

The first time I had come, I had been a stranger, but now I was a friend. It was one of those friendships that changes an acquaintance in a short space of time. Bedtime had been late that first time, too. There we had been—the minister, his wife and I— talking into the wee hours of the morning. They were not just casual things about which we had talked so long together, but spiritual things concerning God's Kingdom.

This evening, however, the living room had been filled with guests after the lecture. Special friends had been asked in for a social time, but also for another purpose. My new friend had sprung that on me as I was having my second cup of coffee.

"I have invited these friends in tonight, hoping that you could repeat the talk we had the last time you were here. Do you remember how you told my wife and me of the things you have prayed about and received an answer? I want you to tell these folks specifically about the time when you could have had a terrible accident and you let go of the wheel and let God take over."

Now I let my mind wander back. How well I remembered our first visit. We had talked about prayer during those hours. I guess I had done most of the talking. They had been such good listeners. Tonight he had extracted, little by little, all those things he

2

wanted me to repeat. I had never realized what a lasting impression the earlier conversation had made. It was two o'clock in the morning before the guests left and then the three of us had lingered for yet another half hour. . . . I went to bed quickly, but I couldn't go to sleep. Thoughts kept racing through my brain. I was tired, I told myself, too tired. I had driven a hundred miles in one afternoon, spoken to a crowd of three hundred people that night and talked until two thirty in the morning. But I knew it wasn't just being tired. It was the joy that filled my heart. A seed had been planted. A book was going to be born because it had been conceived in my heart. I had never thought I would write a book on religious matters. Not that I hadn't wanted to, but with all of today's great, well-educated theologians and philosophers, who was I to state my simple way of thinking and knowing God? Still, I knew I had much to tell that would be helpful to housewives and other lay people. And writing a book like that would be wonderful. It would be like talking, like telling a story.

I remembered how gloriously happy I had been when, early in my married life, I found that I was going to bear a child. Writing a book affected me the same way. I am never happier than when I have one in the making. It is fascinating to watch the words come out of the typewriter. My way of writing is, perhaps, a bit unique. I never do any research, never make any notes, or gather any materials. I just sit down and let the words flow from my mind, knowing they are already written in my heart.

In God's eternity there is no end and no beginning. So in the God-Mind, this book had already been written. All that was left for me to do was to record it. That wonderful knowledge had come to me when I wrote my first book, PAPA'S WIFE, and I used the same method in writing PAPA'S DAUGHTER. I never worried about words. The most important thing was

3

to be still and cut off all thoughts of material things, to focus my mind on God from whom all talents and thoughts came.

It is exciting to write. There is no labor connected with it, rather a relaxed, happy knowledge that word after word will form sentences, and sentences pages, and pages chapters and so on. When the words stop coming, that is the end of my writing, and a book has been born.

But to be still was the most important part, to let the mind rest. Words are like music. They are only so many notes. A person can play them and one knows that they are just notes put together. Ah, but if an artist takes these notes—the very same notes —they come out as living music that laughs and cries and moves all the listening world. All writers use words, but their effect depends on how they are put together. And words given to me by my Heavenly Father, I knew, would come out in beautiful poesy.

And so instead of sleeping, I basked in the wonder of my new thoughts. I was not a theologian, so I must not be preachy. But I could tell in a simple way some of the things God had done for me here in this earth life.

As I thought about this yet-to-be-written book, I remembered all the letters—almost a trunkful—from people who had written to me regarding my two earlier books. They were from many different countries, and of different faiths. Many said my writing had helped them solve their problems. Reading about Papa and Mama and their happy family life had made them realize that God *was* good and that this old world was not such a bad place to live in after all. There were those who had expressed a desire to catch some of that happy, deep faith in God that Mama possessed. I recalled how many letters I had written in answer to those I had received, trying to share some of my own trust and faith in God and life. I hoped that I had set some people walking in the right direction. A book of the kind suggested by my minister friend might be of help to many. I would pray that it would be the type of book that would speak to the heart.

Yes, I would write a book the way I talked. It would be a simple book, so simple that a child could understand it. It would not be too long and would be spiced here and there with a trifle of humor. I would go back into my childhood and pick up the path of my search for God and I knew that I would find on the way gold nuggets that I had missed when I had hastened over that road many years ago. It would be wonderful to recall it all. . . .

And then, as I was thinking, a plan came to me. The things I would tell in my book would be the things I had learned at my Mama's knee, things she had in her gentle way imprinted on my mind as far back as I could remember. Papa had been the preacher, the pathfinder, my ideal, the one I wanted to try to live up to. But it was Mama's way that I had taken. It was her love for people that I had inherited and her love of serving the Lord God. And now, as I walked back through the long corridors of time, I saw how much like Mama I was in the way I prayed and talked and dreamed. So my book would be about Mama's way as I had followed it.

Wasn't it Mama who had told me stories about God as I sat on her lap, stories that had made me see God in nature, that made God a very part of it all? Yes, in my childish mind I had seen God's cheeks puff out as He blew out the wind; His chariot, cleaving the sky in the thunder and the lightning, become a burning snake winding its way to the earth. And it had seemed to me that in the silvery moonlight God was pouring His blessings down on this world He loved so much. Each blessing glided down on white angel wings to transform everything it touched into peace and joy. In the early mornings, when dewdrops were still on the grass, I could feel God walking beside me.

And so often in the cold winter, as I walked through a wood transformed into a white wonderland and stood spellbound at the picture I saw, I felt Him near. Each snow-laden tree and bush looked like a bride kneeling to pray. So it was in the springtime, when the soft fine rain fell on my uplifted face in a gentle caress. Surely the God my Mama had told me about was there. And even autumn did not conceal Him away from my view, for when the leaves had outlived their brilliant color-play and limp and sad singled themselves to the damp ground, it seemed that if I would but listen, I could hear a whisper. God was speaking to His trees, assuring them that this was just for their own good, a time of rest which would enable them to bring forth even more abundant loveliness. And there would be another spring, new life, as soon as the winter was over. And so my heart felt no sadness as the trees disrobed, because His promise was there. God's creation could never die.

How strange life would have been and how empty even now if I didn't believe in Him that way, if I was not assured that He was there beside me. How terrifying would be the thought of bombs and new weapons of destruction if I didn't know, without a single doubt, that the world is in God's hands and He holds the reins and that men can go just so far and no further. Just a whisper from Him and they are gone from this world like a vapor, and they are no more. For life on earth is measured in years and no matter how good or beautiful, how wicked or destructive, people are, there comes an end to their years and only the things that they have done remain.

There came a time in my life when the beautiful, secure picture of God that Mama had given me began to dim. It was in my adolescent years, I remember, that there was doubt and many a question mark as to how God could be. But when the turmoil of those years was over, and that first storm of life had passed, I saw Mama's pathway again and as I began to walk on it, I found that I had mellowed a little because of those confused years. And so, I learned from my own mind things to which my heart agreed, such as, we will our own thoughts through our imagination. In my childhood my imagination and I could travel, taking away the drab and dull, tinting life to any color we wanted it. Even as an adult, this friend has never left me. As a child it was my playmate; as an adult, a mirror of my thought life. Because of it, I came closer to God as I learned to discipline my thought world.

I wanted to live in a happy world, so I willed my thoughts that way. I put a keeper at the door of my mind and let only good, constructive thoughts enter. I became a sort of mystic, and I still am, for I never lost that childhood friend that transformed living into happiness. We are all mystics in those first enchanting years of life. We play train on the kitchen chairs and travel in five short minutes all over the world. We sit on a magic carpet and whisper, "Lift," and we are raised up into the sky. We sail on fleecy clouds and drop in to have a party with the moon man's children. When we return to earth again, we have stardust in our eyes. Don't you remember how you talked to trees and flowers? They were your closest friends. Perhaps you, too, feasted on bark and leaves, served on broken pieces of glass, and believed you were dining in a king's palace. Ours was truly a magic world, filled with wonderment and make-believe. In a world like that, through the mirror of our imagination, it was easy to see God in all the earth.

Oh, there was a time I had said to Mama, "Mama, explain God to me."

And Mama had smiled, that warm little smile of hers.

"How can I explain God to you, my little one?" She looked far into the distance as though she waited for an answer to come from above. "It is like asking me to describe the function of my heart, or to tell the mystery of my brain cells. I know very little of those things. I can't explain them. I only know they are there and that I couldn't live without them. But with God—it's funny I never thought of explaining God. I guess I like to believe that everyone accepts Him just as I do. I know I couldn't exist without His power. Without Him, everything would crumble into nothingness, because all things have their beginning in God's creation. You see, there are so many things we have to accept without having them explained to us."

She sat still for a moment, then continued, with me hanging on to her every word: "Now if you had asked me to explain myself, I would find that even harder to do. Sometimes the questions come to me— Who am I? Where do my thoughts come from? What creates within me such emotions that sometimes I feel as though they would tear me apart and sometimes that they would lift me to the pinnacle of heaven? What creates this joy and sorrow, tears and laughter? The texture of my hair? The way my eyes see and my ears hear? The way I walk with balance and know what to do or not to do? Where was this life in me before I was born? Where do I go when the gates of death swing open for me to enter in? There are more than a million questions that I can't answer even for myself. But this I can say with confidence —I am because God created me. He made me this wonderful way. That is how I exist. That is why I laugh and cry and think and dream dreams. I accept myself because I am—but all because of God. . . ."

So my book would be a book of stories of the way I had walked and of the people I had met, troubled people seeking some lasting values for this life on earth. Perhaps by the telling of those stories, others would be helped. Much of my book would be devoted to writing about the power of prayer. That would be my theme: how God's answers to prayer are beyond what we can ever comprehend. I would share things that had taken place in my own home among members of my own dear family. And so, I thought, I would be able to fulfill my friends' wishes and write a book the way I talked. And it would be born in due time and would carry a message to those who were too busy or too tired to read deeper books on religion. This book would be relaxing and at the same time it would give food to the soul.

For to become balanced persons, three things within us must be fed, the body, the mind and the soul. . . . The body always seems to be taken care of first. It is very demanding. It will not let us forget. If we do, it causes us much pain and discomfort. The mind, too, demands feeding, because it is restless when left inactive. People hunger for fine literature and most homes have books and magazines galore. And it also feasts on plays and radio and television programs and lectures. But the soul is often neglected. It is shy and patient and makes no outstanding demands. If neglected, it cries softly within the heart and we are filled with an anxiety and despair which at times we do not understand. There's that uneasy and lost feeling. If the soul is never fed, it will just wither and crumble into a small unnoticed something. It is a sad thing when a soul that should glow and sparkle is slowly starved into nothingness.

To feed it properly, we must read the Bible and spiritual books, listen to good sermons and go to places of worship. And most of all, we must not neglect prayer. Our prayers should go up all day long, happy prayers full of joy and thankfulness for all the wonderful things God has poured down upon us. If a soul is fed, it is happy, but it has no rest until it rests in God.

How sad that some people think prayer is only to be used when we are in danger or in desperate need of something for ourselves. Prayer is really as necessary as breathing. It is our contact with our Father God, for in Him we live and move and have our being.

Chapter Two

My training to serve God began in the school of prayer, which is the strongest power on earth. As my mind wanders back into my childhood days, and memories unfold as pages in a book, I remember how Mama brought us eight children up on prayer. She served it both as a full-course meal and as snacks in between. There was no escaping from this order. It was the only contact between heaven and earth, so when one wanted to commune with God, one must pray. But some confusing thoughts entered into my childish mind when I discovered the difference between my parents' prayers. Often I wondered which one of them was right and who used the true method to approach God the prayer way.

Mama was impatient in her praying. She was never willing to wait for things, but expected an immediate answer. Papa seemed to leave the outcome up to God. If he could not see an answer, he accepted that as God's wisdom, and no doubt clouded his faith in God's power. Perhaps, I reasoned within myself, it was the things they prayed about that made the difference. To Mama, prayer came as easy as breathing. Even if she knew people termed her prayer method strange and naïve, it never seemed to bother her. She kept on praying that the cake she had placed in the oven would not-fall and that the food would stretch a long way because there were so many to feed at one table. And there was the long line of people who depended on her help and came to ask her to take their problems to God for them. Those people surely believe that God would answer them through Mama. They felt that in some strange way she was "in" with God and that He would grant her what He would refuse them. So prayers would be sent out for a quick sale of their house, for a husband to be kinder to his wife, and children to recover from their colds. I often heard her prayers and saw the people coming, and I never remember one who went away disappointed. Things did change when Mama talked with God.

Of course, Papa, as a minister, had certain prayer projects. His prayers were always sincere as he was himself, and many people came to his study with their prayer problems. Then there were the sickbed prayers where he made his daily calls. Papa's prayers seemed to me loftier than Mama's. They were bigger prayers! Still, when Papa prayed for the man who had a bad case of lumbago and was in pain day and night, he seemed to get worse instead of better. He wasn't healed. And how can I ever forget that lovely wife with a devoted husband and their family of five small children? Knowing she was at death's door, Papa prayed for her all night long. All hope was gone, but my Papa prayed on, torn by fatigue and compassion. But the wife died. Could God answer only small prayers? I wondered. I felt sorry for Papa. I decided I must help restore him to those church members who trusted him. I would tackle something really hard. I would help Papa to pray and give him the credit in the church when the answer came. I chose for my project a man with one leg two inches shorter than the other. Day after day and night after night I knelt and prayed that God would make his short leg grow as long as the normal leg. For a year I believed and watched the man with great expectation and eagerness. But the answer never came; he limped as badly as before. It was so discouraging it pained me. There was something wrong with the way Papa and I prayed. But what?

Then came another discouraging experience. This time it was one of my sisters, who had a panicky fear of the dentist. Having observed Mama's way of talking to God, she hit upon a bright idea. There was no need to tell Mama and Papa that she had a big cavity in her tooth. She would go directly to God and tell Him about it and ask Him to do the work on it. It would be wonderful! There would be no more suffering in that dentist's chair. Mama had always said that nothing was impossible for God to do. My sister decided to try it that very night; she would set forth alone on this prayer adventure.

"Please, please, God," she prayed as she knelt by her bed, "fill my tooth. Fill it good and hard . . . and do the work while I sleep. I want it all filled when I wake up in the morning. Thank you for being so good to me . . . and I shall always try to be a good girl. Amen."

The next morning when she awoke, she slid her tongue over the spot where the cavity had been. It wasn't there—the tooth was filled. She was healed! Breathless with excitement, she rushed out to Mama in the kitchen.

"Mama, Mama," she cried, "God has done it again!"

Mama stopped beating the eggs and gazed with surprise at her young daughter. "He has done what?" she asked.

"He filled my tooth last night, Mama, when I asked Him to. I didn't want to tell you I had a big cavity and that I was afraid to go to the dentist. So I asked God to fill it. Isn't it just wonderful? Now we'll never need to pay money to the dentist again, even if he does only charge us half price."

Mama patted the excited girl on her blonde head.

She asked to be shown the miracle and, equipped with a toothpick, she poked at the tooth. It didn't take her long to come to a verdict. She looked tenderly down at her offspring as she held the toothpick in front of her eyes. "It wasn't God this time, darling." She smiled. "Your tooth was filled with a piece of bread."

I surely felt as though God and Mama had both let my little sister down, but Papa explained some things to us that morning around the breakfast table. And he gave us a clear understanding of how God works through prayer. God was a wise God, he said, and everything in His world was made in order. Dentists had been given their skill by God to help people, and children should be thankful they could go to them when they had a bad toothache. It wasn't that God couldn't . . . it was that He didn't choose to. My sister's prayer had been a foolish, selfish prayer and not one to honor God.

That made me understand another of my child prayers that I had wondered about before. Every Christmas season our church had an auction where things were sold to benefit the poor and needy. Strange as it might seem now, looking back on our strict church discipline, chances were sold to make money. A certain big item was chanced out and, of course, that would be the thing that made the most money. That year it had been a doll. No, not just an ordinary doll. It was a creation! I, who only owned one little rag doll, stood in awe before it. To call a doll like that mine would be like living in heaven. I can't remember anything I ever wanted more than that doll. Jubilantly I watched Papa buy a chance. It was number 8. Then I went aside from the crowd and prayed the most sincere, heartbreaking prayer ever prayed. I promised God everything if He would see that I got that doll, and there was no doubt in my mind as I went back and watched the drawing. Already I felt as though I held the doll in my arms. My heart was broken when number 15 won. And, lo and behold, the prize went to a well-to-do family with a girl my age who already had five beautiful dolls. It was unfair of God, I had been thinking, and I was bitter toward Mary who had so many things. But I had never dared tell Papa that God was not fair. Now Papa's words set me straight. My prayer had been a selfish, foolish prayer. I had wanted something for myself which was not to the honor and glory of God. And so the Lord God again rose to His former height and majesty in my mind. My faith was restored because of my sister's prayer.

Little by little I seemed to grasp more of this strange power that we earth people use to contact God for the good of the world we live in. But still I didn't really know what prayer was until one day I accompanied Papa on a call to an old man's shack on a cold fall afternoon. It was three long miles to his dwelling and Papa and I walked it through the forest. I must have been about nine years old at the time, but how well I remember that walk! It was fun to walk with Papa. He was so big and strong, it gave me an air of importance. I felt very secure having him hold my hand. In my mind Papa was the greatest person on earth. He came next in line to God. Nothing bad could come to me when Papa held my hand.

The man was bedridden, crippled up with aches and pains. His shack was very primitive. He insisted that Papa make coffee for us. So Papa put on the muddy-looking coffeepot and found some cookies, and although they were musty-looking and smelled funny, he ate two. I didn't want any, but one look from Papa made me understand it would be very rude not to eat one. It might hurt the man's feelings. After we had had our coffee and had served the old man some, too, we sat down by his bed and Papa read from the Bible about the lame man that the Master healed. After the reading, we knelt to pray.

Papa prayed first. It was a long prayer. I soon lost track of it and escaped to my own imaginative world. Then, suddenly, Papa nudged me to indicate that I was to pray, too. I meant it from my heart when I asked God to make the man well, and I even thanked God for the musty cooky. After my "amen" there was a short silence and then the man prayed. He clasped his disfigured hands and lifted his face heavenward. Something very special came into his voice, and although it was against the rule, I opened my eyes to peek just a wee bit at him. I couldn't figure it out, but his face changed as he prayed. It was radiant with joy, almost shiny, and my eyes opened wider and wider. That man never asked to be healed. He didn't ask God for anything. He just thanked Him as though he had been given everything in the whole world. He thanked God for the poor little shack in which he lived, for his warm bed, and for the kind people who dropped in to care for him. He prayed for his pastor and the blessing he had brought in coming out to read and pray with him, and even for his little girl who prayed so sweetly. He went on thanking God for the birds in the branches of the big tree outside his window and the snow that soon would come and make the world white; for summer and its beauty and this windy fall day that made him feel snug and sheltered in this room where he was sure of God's protection day and night. I never closed my eyes again during his prayer because I loved to see how quickly he kept changing as he talked with God. When we bade him good-bye, he looked as happy and contented as though he had no discomfort at all. And where before his face had been twisted with pain, it now looked relaxed and joyous.

How could it have happened? I wondered, perplexed. How could words tossed into the air make such a difference? The man was still sick, but that prayer had taken the sadness out of him. I realized that the change must have been within his heart—it was the joy from a happy inside that shone through. On the way home I asked Papa to explain prayer to me. And Papa did his best to try to come down to my level.

"My girl," he said, "prayers are the thoughts that come forth from our inner being. Prayer is our highest self, the very best within us that comes out in words from our lips. For once we are absolutely honest, knowing that we can hide nothing from God. As we pray, we become humble and sincere and there is a desire deep within us to be good. Forming prayer into words makes it more tangible. The words form a contact with God, so that our eyes reflect a glimpse of His glory. The heart beats with joy, for we know in God there is help for all our problems."

I walked silently beside my Papa for a long time. He had talked to me as though I were a grownup, and I was proud and happy. The wind blew in the treetops. It was bitter cold. My feet ached now and I felt as if there were little stones in my shoes. It was getting dark. Papa still held my hand in his. His words are true, I was thinking; prayer must be like that. I had seen it in the old man's face. When he had made the contact with his God, he had forgotten his pain and loneliness. His aches were still there, but he could bear them with courage. Perhaps, I thought, that was a greater answer than to be made well.

"Look, dear," said Papa. "See the lights over there in the village. See, there is the parsonage—Mama just lit the lamp. Soon we will be home!"

It's like prayer, I was thinking, as my heart beat fast in the gladness of this new thought. Prayer is like walking in the dark and suddenly seeing a lamp being lit to tell you home is there. In prayer God is waiting for us, just as in the parsonage Mama was waiting for Papa and me. She knew we would be cold and hungry and tired, and she would meet us with open arms to welcome us home. It would be warm inside those walls, and clean and homey. Good food would be cooking on the stove. Mama would take my shoes off and warm my feet, placing soft slippers on them. I could see it all in my mind as I walked with Papa toward the light.

And so it was with prayer. The sick old man had seen the light of God's world; he had seen his Father's house and knew that he soon would be home. There would be no more sickness or pain or loneliness there, and no more sorrow. And the light of prayer would lead him home.

For the first time I seemed to understand what prayer was good for and why it was the only pathway that leads us from our earth mind to God's Kingdom where all is well. And it wasn't so far to reach; one had only to walk toward that light.

It was as though a big star had appeared in the sky of my limited thought world. God was real! Prayer was not asking selfishly for what one wanted from God. Prayer was contact with a power so great that just one spark from that source would transform things into good.

A little later in life, when I was just about to leave my childhood and step up onto higher ground, I heard from Papa about prayer again. It was when I felt my mind stretching and my thoughts widening and I understood that what counted most in life was the value we set on things and how much we were willing to pay to keep that value.

Papa was sitting at his big desk in his study and I was standing beside him. I was thrilled to be a part of that room, even if I was only a part like the desk, or the Bible, or the picture of The Rich Young Ruler approaching the Master. I was a small part, indeed, but I was there, and Papa put his pen away and leaned back in his chair.

"What am I writing?" He repeated the question I had asked him. "I am trying to explain prayer for the prayer session this week."

"And what did you write, Papa?"

He lifted the white paper from the desk and began to read:

"Prayer is the best in us approaching a Holy God. It is as if we were disrobed of our vanity—our pride—our selfishness. It is the highest honesty in our hearts that truly seeks to adjust to a higher will. It is when we lose self that we find the Christ within and there is the contact made. Prayers have an answer. We are at home in our Father's House. Oh, that we would dwell there forever. . . .

They were like the words he had said before, and I understood what he read. Prayer would be my light to lead me through the unknown years ahead. I would always believe in it because I had seen prayer's answer in the face of the sick old man a long time ago. There was a man who had contacted God and found peace.

As the years went by I understood more and more. It became clear to me that prayer was never an individual thing; it was universal. What we ask for one affects all, because prayer is always answered. It is like a missile shooting through the air into space. It is never lost, but will keep on doing the good it is sent out to accomplish. It belongs to eternity. Somewhere a heavy burden will be lifted, because someone knelt in prayer. A pain too torturing to bear will lose its grip and a heart caught in agony and despair will find sudden rest. Because of prayer, God comes to men. Prayer will find its goal. Our sight is short and we see only so far . . . but far, far beyond the horizon prayer finds its answer through the channel God has directed. What a loss to the world and heaven, too, that so many neglect to pray.

The prayers of those who have chosen to serve God here on earth go before them, as a preparation. And so when contact is made, help comes swiftly and it is as strong as eagle wings. Prayer is the strong, silent partner to those who believe.

Chapter Three

What a difference it makes to know all about prayer, to understand its mystery, and then to try to reach out and touch it. I do sincerely hope that sharing my reaching out will help others to begin to measure the strength of their faith and see how high it stretches into the unknown. I realize now if we know deep within our hearts only a speck of the greatness of our God and can also comprehend this with our mind, we have found the contact. One has to believe in his heart and think with his mind and find that the two will melt into one great and glorious experience, before one can pull the lever that releases the power in prayer.

It took me a long time to realize this in my own mind. Yes, I prayed each day and I believed in my heart that God would and could protect, help and give me strength. But when it came to reaching out and trying it, I was still a babe in understanding.

It was once when Mama came up from Florida to spend a few weeks at our home in Longmeadow that I made my search more intense and, as I really believe, made myself dare to launch out. I was a mother of two grown daughters and I had even held my first grandson in my arms when this came to pass.

Mama was sitting out in the garden reading an article about prayer in a magazine. Sitting in another chair beside her, I had watched her expression as she read. Presently, she threw the magazine aside.

"I can't understand why they make it so complicated, when it is so simple," she burst out impatiently.

"What is so complicated, Mama?" I asked.

"Those things they write about prayer. . . . Why must people feel that they need to go to school to learn to pray, and still hardly dare to believe that they should expect an answer?"

I smiled as I watched the frown on her forehead. If the world only knew that my Mama was an expert in prayer, I was thinking. If they could only know that her prayers always seemed to get an answer with unbelievable speed. Oh, surely the world of today would find her naïve. But did not the Master place a child in the midst of His disciples and tell them that that was the pattern they were to follow in their faith?

"You know, dear," said Mama, "prayer is too simple. That is why some people don't use it more. It is simple enough for a little child to understand. You just ask God . . . or tell Him the problem and *leave it there*. God is ready and willing to take care of all his earth people's needs."

Those three words stuck in my mind: "Leave it there." That was one of our troubles in praying. We carried our heavy burdens to the Lord, sometimes with the help of others, and after placing them humbly at His feet, we picked them up again and continued to carry the load. That was what made Mama so happy after she had prayed. She had left whatever it was she carried—for herself or for others—left it right there with God—sure that it was in His hands now. She could relax and rest, knowing that the answer was on its way.

We did not talk about the subject any more. There were busy days as always in a happy household. I meant to read the article Mama had fretted so about, but I never got around to it. The weeks went by and Mama went back to her Florida and as fall came on,

I started to lecture on my yet unpublished first book. Driving and speaking kept me busy. There was a glow within me, as I waited for some publisher to accept the book. I felt this newborn babe was a gift from God. My childhood dreams had finally been fulfilled, and my heart held great hopes. And so came a night when I, for the first time, took Mama's advice to pray and leave it with the Lord God.

It might seem like a silly prayer, but I offered it on the spur of the moment, and with as much sincerity as if I prayed for the greatest cause in the world. And it wasn't just the small thing I asked protection for that mattered. The thing that counted was that the answer did come.

I was returning home from a two-hundred-mile speaking trip. It was a cold November day. The trees were disrobed and the glory and beauty of autumn were all in the past. It was that time of year when the earth seems a little dreary and when you long for the soft white blanket of snow to fall and cover it up until spring comes again. I was tired! I had spoken to a large woman's club group and, as always, I had been asked when my book was to be published. I still had no answer. If I had but known that Rinehart & Company would take it a month later, in December, I perhaps would not have noticed the bare, bleak world. But I was a bit depressed. In Springfield I stopped on a busy street to go into a drugstore. I slid out on the right side of the car to avoid holding up the stream of traffic. It was only when I reached home that I noticed my little blue velvet hat was missing. It began to come clear to me how it must have happened. The hat had been beside me in the front seat of the car, and I had evidently pushed it off the seat into the street when I went into the drugstore. It was a good hat and one of my favorites. Furthermore, it had been bought to go with my lecturing dress and I just couldn't lose it. My first impulse was to drive back and see if it was still there, crushed, of course, with all that traffic. Nevertheless I wanted it, and perhaps it could be restored.

But I was very tired and weary. I had had a long ride and home seemed so good with its light and its happy voices. Outside it was dark and cold and I had already put the car in the garage. And so, the thought came to me . . . perhaps it wasn't even right to ask God about it, but I would. I would do what Mama had told me; I would pray to God to protect my hat until morning and just "leave it there" with Him. I can't remember if I spoke the words out loud, or if they just came from my heart, but this is what I felt:

Father God, I don't know if this is an orderly prayer; if it isn't, forgive my foolishness. But I think of you as my wonderful heavenly Father, and I want to talk to you as a child would talk to his parent. Tonight I am like a little child holding up a broken toy, asking you to fix it. You know all about my little hat lying there on the busy street. It is a good hat and I should be concerned about it. Please, Father, protect it for me until morning. I thank you with all my heart.

Amen

I went to bed early and had a good night's sleep. I forgot about the hat during the night, wanting so to follow Mama's suggestion to "leave it there." About eight A.M. I was ready to drive back and pick it up. My younger daughter wondered where I was heading so early in the morning. And when I told her, she just sat down on a chair and laughed to her heart's content.

"Mommie," she cried, "you do the funniest things! No one but you would ever believe that a thing like that could happen. How in the world can you expect the hat to still be there? And if it is, it surely wouldn't look like a hat by this time."

I assured her that I knew what I was doing,

and I expected to be able to show her my hat when she came home from high school that afternoon. When we parted, she still had that funny smile on her face.

"I am sure it will be all right!" I kept saying to myself as I drove along. There was a calmness in my heart and an anticipation that excited all my other emotions.

I parked the car in the same place as I had the night before and slid out just as I had done then. And when I looked down at the street, there it was—the little blue velvet hat, as nice and fresh as if it had just come out of a hatbox. For a moment I held it in my arms and hugged it gently as though it were a child. Tears rolled down my cheeks.

"Thank you, Father God," I whispered. "You did care and You did hear my prayer. I just don't know how to thank You."

It was a miracle! And it surely was to the Glory of God because I felt my faith grow and vision widen. Cars had been coming and going all night. They had been driving an inch in front of the little blue hat and an inch in back. They had parked beside it and missed it by an eighth of an inch. How many times it must have been in danger of being crushed, but it had been protected. If God could care enough to protect a little hat, how much more would He care to protect me as I traveled on the busy highways. A warm, gentle feeling encompassed my heart. I had touched prayer in a strange way, and it was wonderful!

You might ask me: Do I recommend that people pray for God to take care of things they do not feel like doing themselves? No, I don't! It is important for a prayer like this not to be minimized, or made fun of. I believe that we should pray from our own hearts for whatever need is there. But we must be true to our own selves, and not try to copy others. We are all individuals and we will have to agree to disagree on many things. But we must not take from each other the uniqueness of personal faith. I knew I had done a thing that Mama would have done. Papa would have thought it a silly prayer, although, I know, he never would have doubted God's power to answer it. God sees in our hearts what we are. It is not what we ask, it is the sincerity and the trust that flows out of a trembling heart that our God honors. A lark, could it pray, would not ask to swim under water; and could we picture a perch—if a fish could pray— asking that it be able to sit in the treetops and sing? No, we know that it would only be right for the lark to pray that it could sing more beautiful songs and soar higher and higher in a blue sky, and for the perch that it could swim in deep, clear water. So it is with us. That prayer was true to my nature, and that is why God honored it. And my faith grew, because I was naïve enough to believe in it with both my heart and mind and leave it to God's will. Some people could never pray a prayer like that and feel right about it. And they should be admired and honored for their high ideals. But let us be ourselves. That is the way we can best serve our God here on earth. How clear that became in my mind, and how much I needed that lesson! Praying was just like learning to float. What a time I had until I really felt that if I threw myself on the water and trusted it, it would bear me up. But if I was frightened and didn't dare to let go of myself, I would sink.

The next lesson that I was to learn concerned the prayer of intercession, when someone else prayed to God for my protection.

Again I was on a lecturing trip. My first book had been published and was a great success. I was happy and grateful and my lecturing now stretched far and wide. This time I was returning home from Portland, Maine, where I had spoken to a large club. I had been invited to spend the night with a minister friend and his lovely wife who had a little cottage by the ocean. Those were the highlights of my traveling, the wonderful dear friendships I made and the warmth I felt from being wanted. God was so gracious to me. He knew how I loved people and now I was meeting fine and noble people, adding day by day to my long list of earth friends.

It was February, and the ocean was stormy. I think I shall always hear in my mind those waves rolling in and out against the rocky shore that night. The ocean sang the lullaby that rocked me to sleep, and in the morning I awoke refreshed and rested and ready to start my journey home. First, we had breakfast in a dining room with windows on three sides looking out on the ocean. There was a glow around the table, a glow of love and fellowship. The minister read aloud from the Bible and shared with us some of the deep thoughts from his daily five A.M. meditations. The room was filled with a humble, sweet spirit. As we parted we clasped hands in prayer.

"The radio is forecasting a big snowstorm," said the pastor. "You better get going. Drive carefully and God be with you."

As I kissed my hostess good-bye she clung to my hand, lifting her face in prayer:

Dear God—protect her. Don't let anything happen to her. And lead her safely to her loved ones.

Her sweet sincerity was still ringing in my ears as I drove toward home. God was so good to me and the world was full of wonderful people.

I had only gone about thirty miles when the storm began. It started slowly, but became worse and worse. It was sleeting and freezing and it was hard to keep the car on the road. But I drove slowly, trying to remember that each mile brought me a bit closer to home. It was on Route 128 that it happened. A big truck had been in front of me for miles and miles, and the traffic moved fifteen miles per hour. I am impatient by nature and after a while this got the best of me. If only I could get by that truck, the long line in back of me could get going, too. Looking for an opportunity to pass, I came to a place where the road looked fairly smooth. Even if it was slippery, I would try to get by that big thing. So I stepped on the gas and got the speedometer up to thirty miles. I was halfway by the truck, when I realized my foolishness. But others had pulled out in back of me; I had to make it. The car slipped and skidded and when I was almost past the truck, I lost control of the car. I began to spin around and panic seized me. This was it, I thought. This was the way it felt to have an accident. Would I crash into the truck? Would other cars pile up? Would this be the end? "Please, God, let my husband think to cancel my speaking engagements." Would I land in the hospital? Would I die just in my glory with a successful book out? My thoughts were racing at lightning speed through my brain and then the calm. . . . It was only seconds— but again I was back in that cottage by the ocean. I saw my friend lift her face, asking God to protect me. And somehow I knew that that prayer had gone with me and it was here now to do its work.

"I can't drive, Father," I called out. "Take the wheel."

The next thing I knew, I was sitting on an uphill bank by the road, the car facing the opposite direction. The kindly truck driver stood beside me. All traffic had stopped. His truck was zigzagged across the road. Another truck behind him had parked across the road, too, to stop all traffic from trickling through.

"It was a miracle," said the truck driver. "How could you get control of the car and drive it onto the bank just when I was sure we were crashing? You were two inches from me, Lady. You gave me the worst scare I've ever had."

But I couldn't answer. How could I tell him I hadn't driven the car, that I had let go of the wheel and let God take over? Would he understand if I said prayer had protected us? Finally my voice came. "I prayed," I whispered. "I was foolish to try to pass, but I didn't want to hurt you, too."

"You surely did something!" he gasped.

My head was as light as a feather. I felt unreal. Perhaps I was dead after all, I was thinking, and it just felt as if I were alive. But the kind driver and another truck driver took the car down from the bank and made me walk around a little to get some exercise. Then they drove after me, asking me to stop at the next restaurant for a cup of coffee. They didn't leave me until they were sure I felt strong enough to drive on. I shall never cease to wonder about their kindness and concern. Although I never found out their names, I shall bless them forever.

What an experience that was! Now I never start off on a drive in my car without lifting my face in this prayer:

Father,
   Help me to drive so I won't endanger others, and others to drive so they won't endanger me. And take the wheel and drive with me, so I can feel completely protected.

And then I start off. Whether my drive is long or short, I know that prayer will protect me from harm.

As time went on and I grew in faith, I realized more and more how powerful prayer was. If only all people knew that, I was thinking. How we could pray "big" prayers for our world. We could whisper them through the whole day—prayers filled with love and concern—left in God's care. But soon I was really to be tested on my beliefs in a way I had never expected.

Sickness had come to us! My dear husband had collapsed one day and had been rushed to the hospital for an emergency operation on his stomach. His small

Tool & Die Company was only a couple of years old, and he had not as yet gotten on his feet financially. But he had been struggling along, trying to meet the bills and working as hard as he could. He had only a few men on the payroll besides himself. But money had to come each week to meet that payroll. When he became ill, there was no income and it would be months and months before he could go back to work again. Besides that there were private nurses around the clock and what money we had was dwindling away at a rapid pace. I had had to let the men go and turn the key in the closed door of the shop. If my husband got well, the shop had to be there waiting for him. I knew that would have everything to do with his recovery. Although I didn't know just how, I knew I must keep up the rent on the shop or ask for credit. One night with tears running down my cheeks, I sat down to write to all the creditors, telling them how things were and why the bills were not paid. People might say that the world is hard when you are in trouble and that business is business, but I have never had such kindness and understanding come to me as from those business firms. Every creditor answered my letter most graciously, telling me not to worry. They would be happy to put the bills aside until my husband was able to open his shop again. I was amazed at such kindness, but not one of them sent us a bill during all those months. Some even wrote and asked if they could help.

It was surely a joy when he was able to open the shop again and get his men back. He could not work, but he could supervise. And if money came in so he could pay those men, we would soon be on the go again. Things went fine for a couple of weeks and then came one week when some money we had counted on wasn't paid on time. We needed three hundred dollars to pay the men their weekly wages, and there was no money to be had. You can't send a man home to tell his family that there just was no pay.

What were we to do? I shall never forget that September day when my husband came home for lunch with a strange blank look on his face. I guessed the trouble before he told me.

"The money did not come," I said.

"You are right. Not a penny—what shall I do?"

Well, what should he do? We had borrowed from the bank all that we could. There was no one we could ask for money, when all we had was bills and more bills. Presently a smile came to my husband's face. He placed his finger under my chin and lifted my face toward his.

"I know what we will do," he said. "Remember that faith of yours that you can ask God for anything when you are in trouble and He will look out for you? Now I expect that faith of yours to go to work. If it is real, money should rain down on us from Heaven, shouldn't it?"

I nodded, forcing a smile and trying to look unconcerned. But I was scared. I had said those words many times, tossing my head with assurance when he had kidded me. I knew my faith was real. God would help if we asked Him. But hadn't we prayed right along for money to come in time? Why had not God answered us before this? And now, there were only two hours before the bank closed—only two hours. Would God work that fast?

My husband went and sat down in the garden with his newspaper, while I prepared his sandwich and coffee and carried them out to him. I couldn't eat myself. As yet, I had not prayed. I didn't know just how to pray or what to ask. I stood in the kitchen looking up at the blue sky and the bright sun. It was warm for September, the flowers in the garden were in bloom.

"God," [I whispered.] "Father God, I don't even need to tell you, but money must come in time to get into the bank. I don't know how you are go-

31

ing to do this, but I am asking you and leaving it with you. Here, take this heavy burden. I shall not take it back. I know my faith is real. Prayer is power. I know you will not fail me."

Presently a name came to my mind. It was the name of an old friend, but she was not a wealthy person. She worked part time as a cook for a rich household. Whatever made me think of her? Time and time again, her name came to my mind. Was I suppose to get in touch with her? If so, how would she get three hundred dollars and would she be willing to let us have it for a while? I went to the phone and called her place of work. It was her day off and she was not there. I called her daughter's home. No, she was not there. Her daughter expected her, but not until four o'clock. She was downtown shopping.

I was about to hang up when the daughter called out, "Wait a moment, I see Mother coming up the walk now. You can talk to her."

Then my friend was on the phone. My heart almost failed me. But I gathered all the courage I had and asked her straight out, could she possibly lend us some money?

"Yes," she answered quickly in a strange voice. "Come over to my house in a half an hour. I'll be waiting for you."

We drove to her house. "Did you tell her how much we needed?" asked my worried husband.

"No," I confessed, "but she said we could borrow some money."

"How could she be carrying that amount of money in her pocketbook?" he ventured, looking at me as though I could solve the problem with some more words.

We drove the rest of the way in silence. "I mustn't worry. That's taking the burden back," I lectured myself. "I must know that this is the answer."

She was sitting on her front porch when I came up the steps. "How much do you need?" she asked simply.

"Three hundred dollars," I said so softly that I could hardly hear my own voice.

She opened her pocketbook and counted out the money. "Go quickly, so you can get to the bank before it closes," she said.

I thanked her with tears in my eyes, but one more word. "How did you happen to have it?" I asked.

"I will tell you that the next time I see you. There is no hurry about returning it," she assured me. "Use it as long as you need it."

I placed the money in my husband's lap. "Money from Heaven," I whispered as I threw myself in his arms.

He never forgot that day, and from then on, he never doubted what prayer could do, or that God surely cares for us and is willing to help when we ask Him.

Later the lady told me herself how she came to have that money in her pocketbook just when we needed it.

"I was walking around downtown shopping," she said, "when suddenly something like a voice speaking within me urged me to go to the bank and draw out some of my savings. Unable to get the thought out of my mind, I drew the three hundred dollars. I was sure one of my children had been in an accident and needed it. So, I left my shopping and drove straight to my daughter's house. When I arrived and heard your voice, I knew that it was God's voice I had heard, and that I was to help you."

This made a lasting impression on all three of us. Nothing like that had ever happened to her before, and she counted it a privilege to be used by God to answer a prayer.

It was so easy for me to pray after that, whether about big things or little things, because I knew God was closer to me than my own heartbeat and nearer to me than my own breath. Why should we fret and worry and be unhappy, when we have a God like that, who is our Father?

Then came one night when I was driving my daughter to her home, which is about twelve miles from mine. It was a foggy night and the fog seemed to get thicker every minute. As we went up a steep hill and reached the summit, it became simply impossible to see where the road went. By inching ourselves forward, we finally made it downhill again where we could see just enough so we didn't drive off the road. When I was to drive back home, I was really frightened. How would I be able to make that hill? But then I remembered prayer. My fear vanished, for I knew God would be with me.

"Thank you, Father, for your protection," I whispered, as I started out. Just as I reached the foot of the hill and began to climb, a big truck came behind me. Its bright lights dented the fog and I was able to get over the hill. Again I knew that if I only remembered that wherever I was, God was, I need not fear. For there was not one situation that my God could not handle.

Yes, I have prayed about almost anything and now I feel very much like my Mama. Things I found strange that she should pray about, I was praying about myself. And I can now understand her assurance and perfect trust in God.

One night I was in Chicago on a speaking trip. It was midnight and I was changing trains for Lincoln, Nebraska. I had two heavy suitcases and my portfolio to carry. There was only five minutes between trains and a long way to go. There were no redcaps or any help that night, just passengers pushing away, trying to get ahead of each other. On top of that it was raining, a cold drizzle. How can I ever make it? I was wondering, as I struggled on through the night, feeling very much alone and tired. I just had to make that train to be in Lincoln in the morning. My arms seemed to give way—when suddenly, like a warm glow from a fire, the thought came to me: How foolish I am. God will help me. Didn't He always help me when I asked Him? I put down my heavy suitcases. "Father, God," I whispered, "help me to get there in time. I just can't make it myself."

Presently a man came out of nowhere, it seemed, and stood beside me.

"May I help you carry those bags?" he asked. He took my suitcases and I told him which track I had to go to and we made it right on time. He carried them right on the train and before I had time to thank him, he was gone.

I have told these things to the glory of the wonderful God I am serving. Surely He has a plan for me in this earth life. I was trained enough now to begin my work of helping others, ushering them into a new thinking and a stronger faith where they would learn, too, to touch this magnificent power called "prayer."

Chapter Four

There are great men called to preach the word of God from beautiful sanctuaries where there seems to be a holy atmosphere fitting the worship place of God. Others are called to be missionaries in remote countries, far from civilization. And there are some who feel the call to witness to their own families and neighbors in their own home towns. But now and then we find a person who has only the deep desire to try to be a light for his God wherever he is, and to do God's bidding at the right moment, to the right person, whenever the call comes.

It was my desire to listen to God's voice and be of help whenever I felt that call, which I heard so clearly in my heart. Never was it a planned thing. Suddenly and unexpectedly, I found myself talking to people concerning things greater than ourselves. And I knew it was a call because the person I was led to speak with was always trying to find happiness.

One of the dearest women I know I met in one of our city's big department stores when I was buying a coat. The coat needed a little altering and this lady was the fitter who was called in to do the job. Her hands were nimble and she worked quickly, looking up at me every now and then to make some casual remark about the coat, the weather, or any small talk that had very little meaning, when suddenly she put her pincushion down and stood up beside me.

"You know," she said, "day after day as I've pinned up coats and let them down, I've always hoped that someday I would meet a person who was different from the crowd. This life gets so monotonous sometimes. Lady, you are different! Will you tell me why?" She looked at me with great expectation and I gave her a little smile, having been taken by surprise at her remark.

"If I am different, perhaps it is because I am on the top of the world," I said gaily. "You see, I just had my first book published. Another thing could be that I love life and people. Sometimes I can't wait to live each new day. And when I think how wonderfully special God is, I bubble over with joy. Perhaps it comes out and spills over."

"It surely does," she told me. "You are the happiest person I've ever pinned up a coat on. Tell me, why is God so special to you?"

"Isn't He special to you?" I asked.

She shook her head. "I don't think God even knows that I exist."

Before I left the store that afternoon, she had promised to accompany me to a lecture I was giving that same night. At eight o'clock that evening I picked her up outside her apartment house and we drove off as though we had always known each other. . . .

"I loved your talk on 'Mama and Papa,'" she confided in me on the way home, "but that was not why I went with you tonight. I want you to tell me more about God."

We talked late into the night. She was lonely and was carrying some heavy burdens and thousands of worries about the future. We talked many times after that and when I went to a retreat the next fall for a bit of spiritual growth, she came with me. Here, it seemed, she found what she was seeking and that retreat changed her life. She became radiant with a joy that often rubbed off on those whose coats she pinned

up. For she had found her place at the table of the
Lord and her hungry heart had found the food it
needed. And I had gained a friend so loyal and fine
that I shall always be thankful that we met that day
I bought a coat.

It is a simple little story, but helping someone lost
and bewildered to find the light is such a joyous task
that I wouldn't exchange it for all the money in the
world.

It was summer with all its sunshine and laughter!
Happy church people had gathered at a conference
held in beautiful, historic Northfield, Massachusetts.
I was one of the group sent as delegates from the
church to which I belong. But I had also come for a
rest and to strengthen and refresh my own spiritual
life. I hoped to bring back with me a fine report as a
result of the inspirational truths I was to glean from
those ten days.

I named her "The Silent Lady" and I don't think I
have ever seen a mature woman so beautiful. But she
avoided all of us. And when someone tried to reach
out to her in friendship, she would dismiss the person
with a polite, but cool smile. As I watched her day
after day, my heart ached for her. Why is she so
lonely? I wondered. And why doesn't she want
friends?

Every day she took long walks. I saw her start off.
She walked slowly, but with a certain unusual grace.
Her head was held high and she had perfect poise. I
felt the call to speak. But how do you approach a person who does not want to be near anyone and who
carries the sadness of all the world ingrained in her
features? She had soft long golden hair which surrounded her velvety cheeks like a crown of glory. Her
eyes were blue and wistful. They were dreaming
eyes that seemed to look and still not see, eyes that
looked as though she cried into her pillow at night.

Although she was physically tall and stately, there was something small and helpless about her personality.

There must be a story behind that face, I was thinking, a sad heartbreaking story. I must see if I can help her. After all, a servant of God is always on call, regardless of whether it is vacation time or not. So one afternoon when I saw her going off for her walk, I waited fifteen minutes and then I took the same road she had taken, knowing that sooner or later we were bound to meet. We did! I saw her coming around the bend toward me and also saw the expression on her face when she knew she would have to meet me. Just as we met, I stopped.

"May I accompany you back to the dining room?" I asked. "I was just about to turn back. What a glorious day! And isn't Northfield one of those unusual places where you feel as though you were stepping on sacred ground?"

I had turned and was now walking beside her. She smiled back at me, but did not answer my flow of words.

We walked silently for a few moments and then I spoke again, at the same time sending up a little prayer that God would give me the wisdom to say the right thing.

"I don't want to be rude," she suddenly burst out, "and I hope I don't seem ungrateful for your kindness, but I came up here to be alone."

"I had a feeling that was the case and believe me I don't want to force my friendship on you, but somehow I can't get you off my mind. You look so sad, as if you were carrying a heavy burden. How I wish that I could help you!"

"I don't think anyone can help me," she answered sadly, "but I am touched by your thoughtfulness. You see, just now I am trying to run away from life."

"Oh, that is too bad. Life can be so beautiful!"

She smiled a bitter little smile. "For some people,

40

yes, but never for me. I lost my mother whom I adored when I was very young, and my sister became like a mother to me. I clung to her because she was all I had. My father never knew what it was to be a parent. But at the age when I needed my sister the most, she died of that dreadful cancer. I, too, died a little inside every day during her long suffering. But there was nothing I could do to help her, or to keep her. I think that was why I married so young. I needed security. But getting married was the worst tragedy of all. You see, I married a man much older than myself. We were different in every way and as the years went by I became more and more afraid of him. Just recently I left him, but he will not let me go. I thought that at a conference like this, with so many people, I could hide from him. But I learned last night that he is here now and registered at the Inn. He might come anytime and force his attentions on me. Who knows, maybe if I cross him too many times, he might even kill me?"

It was a long speech and she stopped, perplexed.

"I don't know why I told you," she cried. "I never tell anyone my troubles. But somehow, right now I am so overfull with worries and anxiety—it is hard to keep it all inside me. Please forgive me for talking like this. I don't know why you want to bother with me in the first place."

I put my hand on her arm. "I want to be your friend," I said simply. "I am sure that God has sent me to help you."

She stared at me. "God!" she almost sneered. "What does God care about what happens to me?"

"You are wrong, my dear. He does care. There is not one person on this earth He is not concerned about. I am sure He wants you to be happy. You know that eyes have not seen nor have ears heard what glory He has prepared for those who love Him."

"I am afraid I don't love Him very much. Oh, I go to church for my daughter's sake. You see, my husband and I are not of the same religion and I have defied him in bringing our daughter up in my faith. That, of course, is half the trouble between us."

"God loves your husband, too. I am sure he also is very unhappy."

"God wouldn't love him if he knew what a devil he is," she snapped.

"Oh, yes," I insisted. "You see, God sees deeper than his deviltry. He sees deep down into his heart. Something has made him that way, and you have to try to think kindly of him."

We talked every day after that. Soon she asked me to walk with her. We sat together at mealtimes and she even went to church with me.

One night we stood together on the top of a hill. The world below seemed very far away. Presently she came closer to me. "Please," she said, "will you tell me about God. I want to be friendly with God the way you are. But I can never be like you."

"Oh yes, you can," I assured her. "You have to learn to pray, to talk to God as your Father. After you have learned this, you will never feel alone again."

"How can I learn?" she asked eagerly.

"You have to talk to God as though you were a little child, a hurt, bewildered child, longing for His love. Just forget you are grown up, forget all the things that have been. You are a little child again, telling your Father your troubles. I don't need to tell you any more, for after you have talked with God like that, you will feel His love and His guidance and I can guarantee one thing: you will be happier than you have ever been, and everything will work out in the right way."

The next morning when she saw me, she came rushing up to me. She did not look shy any more and her face was lit up by a radiant smile.

"Do you know what?" she burst out, talking so fast she could hardly get her breath. "I tried it and it worked. Last night I became like a little child and I knelt by my bed and talked to God as to a Father. I told Him everything, even the hatefulness that seemed to live in me, and all that bitterness. I asked Him to forgive me and to wash my soul clean from all its hurts and resentments. I stayed on my knees a long time. And for the first time in many, many years, I let my tears flow without holding them back. You know, after that I slept so peacefully that when I awoke this morning, my heart was light. I felt as though I loved the whole world. I was glad to be alive, and I know that happiness will come. I can feel it!"

A few nights after that we were sitting together in the chapel with her husband sitting between us. "I got strength to let him come," she had told me. "I feel sorry for him. God will help me to be kind to him, for I know he is a sick man."

And during the service, she leaned forward and whispered to me. "Did you see it? The bird . . . it was flying over the altar . . . a small white bird flying noiselessly about. I think it was God's sign to me. Do you think I saw the Holy Spirit?"

I knew there had been a bird flying in the chapel. I had seen it, too. It flew absolutely without noise. To me, the bird was gray like a little sparrow. But she had seen it white!

"Whatever it means," I whispered back, "it is beautiful. Believe it is whatever your heart tells you."

Her life was changed after that summer. We became the dearest of friends and looking back now, I can see how wonderfully God fulfilled those words I had spoken of her future happiness. Years have passed by since that summer in Northfield. After a short while her husband passed away. She married again, one of the finest men on earth. Her happiness now is like a warm glow that surrounds her whole being. Together the two of them can take their problems to God and together they can worship Him. And I shall never cease to marvel how God leads those who are willing to serve Him in helping others. And I, through that experience, gained one of the most precious friends a person could ever wish for here on earth.

I went to Northfield other summers and it seemed that I was always called to help at least one person there. Once there was a little minister's wife who couldn't stand the prayer laboratory sessions.

"I am almost sick when I get out of them," she told me. "Something is wrong with the whole thing! I shall not attend again."

"If you feel like that," I said, "it isn't because the prayer laboratory has something wrong with it. It is because you have something wrong within yourself."

I don't know why I said those sharp words to her. It was not at all like me, but they had just come out as though no power on earth could hold them back. And she stood there stunned and hurt and bewildered, as though I had hit her with a whip. But I heard my own voice speaking words more kindly now. "You see," it said, "prayer is like a mirror. In it we see our true selves. If the picture is not a pretty one, it hurts. We have no use for prayer, no need for it. Prayer changes things and we don't want to be changed."

The next moment she was in my arms. "Can I talk to you?" she asked. "You are right. There is something wrong with me."

And it was something very, very wrong. She had been a hypocrite and a faker and she hated the very work of her husband's ministry. But we got it all straightened out and today she is one of the dearest, happiest workers in God's kingdom. And she has her own prayer group to help those who need to learn to pray. I shall never forget the big stone where the two of us knelt and asked God to change her life. And I saw the miracle take place as she said, "I felt as if I took off a dirty old garment and put on a beautiful new white one."

We rejoiced together over her happiness and I am sure in God's heaven all the angels were ringing their bells in gladness over a sinner who had repented.

Oh, when I look back through the album of my memories, there are too many to get them down on paper. I turn the pages reverently, for each person that was sent to me got the help God had already prepared for her. I was just a small tool, who said the right word at the right time.

I see, for instance, a young girl I met in a restaurant. She was a violinist and God had bestowed on her a great talent. But she had one handicap. She had a fear of forgetting her music when she played, a fear that her memory would suddenly go blank and when she felt like that, her fingers would stiffen and she would lose her touch.

After talking together for a while, I had asked her to pray about it, and she had said, "I just don't seem to get through to God. You pray for me! If I can think of you praying for me, I might forget my fear."

I promised her that I would remember her in prayer every day. And I asked her to start memorizing Bible verses. "They will give you confidence and you will not forget what you have to remember," I told her. "Whenever I want to be sure to remember, I memorize a long Psalm. Psalm One Hundred and Three was the first one I tackled when I was new at speaking and had an hour-long speech to remember."

"You remembered the whole One Hundred and Third Psalm?" She stared at me.

"Sure, that's not much. Just try it and see."

"Oh, if only I could do it!"

"And when your fingers feel as though they are getting stiff, change your thoughts. Don't let fear come in. Think of God. 'He keepeth him in perfect peace whose mind is stayed on HIM.' Think of God as beauty. Think of a beautiful sunset on a lazy summer night, of a lone bird flying across the sky as the clouds are tinted in azure and gold. Think of a supper table with a dear little family sitting around it, all bowing in evening grace; of a kitten stretched out on a bed, or a dimpled baby asleep in his mother's arms. And of all things, know that where you are, God is."

"I will try it!" she promised.

We parted, but one fall night, later that year, I received a telegram from her. She was to play in a big concert hall. She gave the time of her performance and said, "Think with me on God."

It went beautifully. Her fear now has left her. Her fingers never stiffen. And again I stand amazed before the ways the Lord God leads His own. I, who knew nothing of music, had helped a great musician to find herself. But then—all things work together for good for those who love the LORD GOD.

Chapter Five

A lamp once lit cannot be hid. It will shine out into the darkness and because of it, many will be guided along their way. So when God's light is lit in our hearts, we cannot hide it from the world. Wherever we are, we will shine and because of it many fellow travelers here in this earth life will see more clearly.

As I look back now, I know for certain that many people, even those very close to me, often found my conception of God and prayer a bit odd. Perhaps it was because of the lightness in the way I talked about prayer, the assurance I always had, that when we pray, there is always an answer.

Some people made a joke of my words. They were kind jokes, so I didn't mind too much. I knew they did not understand this new philosophy; not really new, it had been since the beginning of time. I heard people saying something like this: "If we were to be like you, there wouldn't be a thing to worry about. We'd just have to smile and be happy each day and God would take care of all our affairs."

As I said, I knew they didn't mean to ridicule me. For underneath I know they felt that there was something solid and worth while in my approach to God. And in some strange way they perhaps felt I was especially favored by the Lord, and that He, in His goodness, tolerated my strange ways.

But there came times in those people's lives when even my philosophy came in handy and they actually took advantage of it.

Once a Director of Religious Education and a Sunday-school worker, having attended a convention far from our home city, developed car trouble on the way home. It was just one of those times when two women drivers alone on the highway were stuck. It was summer and the weather was hot and muggy. Standing by their car at the side of the road, unable to go anywhere, was not a pleasant thing.

Presently the Director of Religious Education spoke up: "It's too bad our friend, Thyra, is not with us. She would just pray and, presto, out of nowhere a mechanic would appear, drive up to us and say, 'Ladies, may I have the pleasure of fixing your car? It will cost you absolutely nothing!'"

Her friend agreed that that was just what would happen. Thyra wouldn't tolerate being stuck anywhere. God would see that she was taken care of. They stood there another half an hour. Cars swished by them, little cars, big cars, trucks, trailers, until finally they became impatient.

"Let us try praying about it," one of them said. "It's hard for me to believe that God interferes in things like this, but it won't hurt just to try. And we certainly need help!"

They both became serious about it then and reverently bowed their heads in prayer:

Dear God, our friend would ask You to help us if she were here. Now we want to try it. Please God help us out of this predicament, so that we can be on our way before darkness overtakes us. We thank you, God!

Amen

They told me this story themselves. They said that after their prayer it seemed as if a hush came over their surroundings. It was broken by the sound of a car, which, as it approached them, slowed down to a full stop. The driver, a pleasant young man, asked if they were in trouble and if he could be of some assistance. He lifted the hood and fixed the car and they had hardly had time to think before they were on their way again.

"We were so thrilled," they told me. "We want to believe it was our prayer. But, of course, it could have been just a coincidence. But there by the roadside we assured ourselves that it was an answered prayer."

I still smile when I think about their words and their doubt. If an answer to prayer is just a coincidence, what difference does it make if that is the method God uses? Isn't it wonderful to have a coincidence take place each time you pray? A coincidence that happens for the good? And God is good.

I had almost forgotten that incident when something else happened to me. This time I really got scared and I wondered if it was wrong for me always to bare my heart's thoughts when it made people think all sorts of odd things. At first I felt like laughing the whole thing off. It was crazy! I admitted it to myself. But there came a thought of the seriousness with which the man approached me, and although for a few moments I tried to grasp for straws, I did finally find my Father's hand. And I knew, even in this situation, He would lead me to do His will.

It was exactly nine o'clock on a rainy Saturday morning when the superintendent of a church school telephoned me.

"Thyra," he said in a very humble voice, "Thyra, I have a strange request to make of you. I know God always hears you when you pray and now I want you to pray that He will stop the rain and make the sun shine with all its might so the grass will dry."

I must have been quiet for a long time. Thoughts were racing through my brain. Had I, through my way of praying and talking, dishonored the holy name of God? Anyone should understand that you didn't ask God to interfere with the weather. Why, while this man wanted the sun to shine, some farmer might be praising God for the rain.

"I can't pray a prayer like that," I told him firmly. "I don't think God would want us to ask Him to change the weather to suit our own fancy."

"Believe me, my dear, it is a far cry from suiting my own fancy," he hastened to explain. "This is a real need! You know our Sunday-school picnic is set for one o'clock today. Last night we secured all the food and made everything ready that we could. We worked until midnight packing dishes. The church hall can't hold all that crowd of youngsters, and furthermore, there is not another free Saturday in June that we can get that picnic area. And think of all those children who have counted the days to this picnic. Don't you think God cares about children?"

My heart was heavy and for the first time since I had given myself in God's service I wished that people would take their troubles to their minister. How could I ever pray that God would stop the rain?

"You know," he continued, "this morning when I awoke and saw the clouds gathering in the sky, when I heard the weather report for rain all day, I began pacing the floor of my bedroom, wondering what to do. Then suddenly, I remembered what I had heard you tell a group of your Junior Highers—that you never doubted God's power to do anything, and that a prayer prayed in faith could move mountains. I have never gone in for that sort of thinking, and praying, I'm sorry to say, has not been in my daily routine. But this morning I felt like praying. I knelt down and prayed as I had in my childhood. And I am not ashamed to tell you that tears came to my eyes as I asked God to forgive my thoughtlessness about serving Him. And I begged that He would hear my prayer and let it be a pleasant day. I had a strange feeling He heard me. But because you seem to know Him so well, I want you to add your prayers to mine. It says in the Bible that where two or three ask in His name, it shall be granted."

That did it. I, too, was sure that God had heard his prayer, and I surely could not refuse to add mine to his.

The clouds lifted. The sun came out and it turned out to be the most beautiful day we could have wished for. All the people on that picnic were completely unaware of the prayers that had gone up for the afternoon, and of how gloriously they had been answered.

I couldn't help but wonder how Papa would have regarded that prayer. Perhaps to him it would have sounded like an unorderly one, but God certainly set it in order. And because of it, a man had acquired a new faith in God and joy had filled his heart. He knew now that God was real and that He does listen when His earth people pray, listens and smiles down on them in a glory and power greater than the sun.

That incident touched me deeply. I knew if I told people about it, they would probably say that it just happened, that the weather often changes suddenly and that it would have turned out that way, prayer or no prayer. But that man and I will always know in our hearts that both of us had touched prayer in a tangible way, unseen by human eyes, unbelievable to some people, perhaps, but it had made our faith in God grow to new height.

Yes, this faith is a strange and mysterious thing, but underneath it is a power greater than the atom. If the leaders of the world today would lay aside all their resentments toward each other, and seek the power of prayer, which is God's gift to men, as diligently as they do atomic power, they would find a solution to all their problems. If wardens in prisons, doctors, and ministers all over our world would embrace it, the world would change in the twinkling of an eye and became that paradise God intended in the beginning of time. Perhaps a decade from now the world will wake up! But if that is to happen, I know it will only be if those who have faith pass it to others. That is the only way it can be received. You catch it as you catch the measles and when you have it, you really have it! And what a blessing if believers would radiate this spiritual power so that an epidemic of prayer would spread all over the world.

Sometimes you never have to say a word about it, you just live it. A woman who worked for me in my household told me one day that she had caught it by being in my home.

"I had a great problem," she confided in me. "There was something that had happened and I didn't dare to tell my husband. Watching your way of praying about things, I knew I could do it, too. So one day I knelt on the living-room floor, right beside the vacuum cleaner and prayed that God would take this problem and solve it. And you know, my husband put it off with a smile. I had never known that prayer could be so powerful."

Prayer works for all problems, your own and those of others. I want to tell you about a friend I made, again on a summer vacation in the mountains. She was a darling person in her thirties, with sparkling brown eyes and a winning smile. The management planned many things for the guests to do together, and I enjoyed her company. But gradually, I saw her slipping away from me. A certain man with an ailing wife had attracted her attention. One day when I didn't go on a planned trip, but stayed home to write, this man's wife, who also had remained behind, came to see me. She was in tears.

"Forgive me if I bother you," she sobbed. "I have to talk to someone and you seem so kind and, as a writer, I know you understand people. I hope you can help me."

I left my typewriter and we walked down by the lake.

"I am losing my husband," she blurted out. "Losing him to that friend of yours, the one with the eyes. He has fallen . . . and I know he will leave me. How can I stop him?"

It was a lovely peaceful day and I tried my best to calm her down. There is little one can say in such a case. I had seen it with my own eyes and I was a little afraid of the outcome. Then I remembered my calling and that no problem was too big for God. I promised I would try to convince the young lady how wrong it was to take a husband from his wife. With that she left, still crying as she walked to her cabin.

I spent most of the morning by the lake, meditating. I didn't worry any more. I knew if I could be still in my own heart, knowing that God was God, the right solution would come.

The next day I made it a point to go boating with my friend. After a while I let go of the oars and let the boat glide by itself and I started to talk about prayer. We had talked about it before, so the subject was not new to her. I also told her frankly what I had observed and I asked her if she was interested in this married man. She admitted willingly that she was.

"I'm not in love with my own husband any longer," she said, looking up at me with large wistful eyes. "Our married life is very monotonous. We have grown out of words. There is not even anything to talk about any more. Our children are the only thing that holds us together. Sooner or later we will part. And this man is tired of his ailing wife. He is a wonderful guy! Isn't it better that two are happy than four miserable?"

I knew I was treading on dangerous ground. A home was at stake. No, not one—but two homes. My heart prayed as my mind searched for the right words. But before I had time to say anything she spoke again.

"It was like electricity," she smiled. "When we met and looked into each other's eyes, well, we just knew we belonged together . . . that's all."

"How was it when you met your husband for the first time?" I asked. "Tell me a little bit about the time way back there when you two fell in love."

"Oh, it was very romantic then! I was sure we had enough love to last through eternity. Funny, I never thought then I could ever look at another man."

So she told me their story, a lovely romantic story of how two young people met and fell in love and got married. When she was through, she sat very quietly for a long time. Her eyes were sad. "Oh, those first years we were so happy! Life was wonderful! What do you think happened to us?"

"You didn't keep the fire burning," I answered. "You see love has to be fed. It has to be cared for. It is a precious, delicate thing, which is hurt and bruised so easily that it can lose its beauty. And without attention, understanding and most of all tenderness, it dies."

"Yes," she admitted, "ours did. It died."

"Would you want it back?" I asked softly.

"Oh, if I could have my husband back the way he was when we were first in love—if he could be the same once more—I would be the happiest woman alive. I hate this business of stealing someone else's man. . . . I don't want his wife to suffer. It is just that I want so much to be happy. I have so much to give."

"Then," I said, "before you really give up your own husband and break up a home, couldn't you try to fall in love with him again? I am sure the old feeling is there still. Sometimes love is not dead, it is only covered over with hurts and neglect and bitterness. Why don't you go home and make up your mind to win your own man again? If you have the power to make this man fall for you, I am sure with the same tactics you could win your husband back."

"Do you think I could?" she asked, breathless with excitement.

"I shall pray for you every day, if you will promise me you'll try."

We parted the next day. She packed her suitcase and went home. She was a dear person, a little mixed up, but with an intelligence and ambition found in few.

I didn't hear from her until Christmastime when I had a long letter bubbling over with news. It had worked! She and her husband had found each other again and now their love was deeper than ever. And she was sure it would last because now it was based on the prayer that God would help them to be tender and understanding in the years ahead.

Following one of my lectures, I spent a weekend in a minister's home. It was a typical parsonage with the busy life of church duties: people calling, food to cook, children to attend to. At nighttime a very exhausted minister's wife tried to entertain me in her living room. Her face showed strain and anxiety and I noticed that her words did not come very easily. Suddenly, without warning, she placed her head in her hands and burst into tears.

I tried to comfort her, perplexed at what could have brought this on. She raised her head and tried to smile through her tears.

"Forgive me," she said, "I'm just tired!" She was quiet a moment, fighting to win control of her feelings. "No, it's more than that. I am a hypocrite. I hate being a minister's wife. Most of all, I hate this big old parsonage. We always live in tumble-down old places that are as big as arks. Other young people have nice new homes with shiny kitchens, but you've seen that dump of a kitchen I have to work in. I hate the kitchen most of all."

"Why don't you ask God for a shiny new kitchen?" I asked her.

She stared at me through her tears.

"God doesn't just give away shiny kitchens," she almost snapped. "Oh, no, this is my lot, and I will have to bear it. . . . I'm sorry and ashamed of my outburst, but sometimes I have to explode. There is no one to whom I can tell these things."

"I am glad you told me," I said. "But I still think that God would want you to have a shiny kitchen. You labor hard in His vineyard. Let's pray about it."

I took her by the hand and we walked out into the kitchen. Then we bowed our heads and I prayed a simple prayer, asking God to give her her heart's desire.

Two months later I received this letter from her:

Dear Friend,
Thank you for praying for me and thank you for coming into my life when I was at my lowest ebb. You did more for me than you will ever know. Every day since you left two months ago, I have prayed that God would see that I got a shiny kitchen to work in. It seemed that that was what really would make me happy.

But as I was praying day after day, something seemed to happen to me. I was slowly changing. I began to think about my dear husband and how hard he worked, never asking anything in return for his long hours except to serve God. I saw that I was making his work twice as hard for him with all my complaints. It came to me how I had known when I married him that I could never have things that other young people possessed. I had known it wouldn't always be easy to be a minister's wife. We had been very unhappy of late. With every beautiful new home we were invited to, I had come home full of bitterness and resentment. I was so full of it that I was actually ill. Then you came and spoke to us in our church and later to me alone. You took me in your arms and made me believe that God cared. I know now that God must have sent you. You made me believe in God's abundance and I really began to have faith that I could somehow get a shiny kitchen in this old parsonage.

But as I was praying, a thought came to me. I was not so shiny myself. Perhaps I'd better pray that I was made over first to fit that new kitchen. After that the kitchen did not seem so important. I asked God to take away my self-pity and forgive me my ungraciousness. And He did! I even didn't mind my dull kitchen. But—well, I know this is no surprise to you, but it is a miracle over all miracles to me. I have my shiny kitchen! The trustees of our church decided to modernize our kitchen for a Christmas present. And it is beautiful—fluorescent lights—cabinets—stainless steel sink—new tile floor—everything I had dreamed of. And I had never even hinted I wanted it. But the most important thing is that I am made over, that happiness has returned and that I now believe that nothing is impossible for our God.

Thank you again for coming to help me get my feet on the right path again. God bless you always.

What more is there to say? It's just as Mama proclaimed. God does more than we dare think because He loves us as a Father.

Chapter Six

Many honors have been bestowed on me since I became an author and I have felt unworthy of them, but grateful for the joy they have brought me. I have been a speaker in universities and at various conferences and there was the summer of 1956 when I traveled back to Sweden and had the honor of an audience with Queen Louise. As I sat there in the beautiful blue living room of her summer palace in Skåne, the thought came to me: Can this really be me, that same little girl who dreamed of becoming an author so many, many years ago? Was it I sitting here talking face to face with the Queen of my homeland? Indeed, it was an honor that only God could have made come to pass.

But there was one honor I received that is above all others. It is the one I hug to my heart, and although it pains me a little, I shall keep it there always and be forever thankful that it came to me.

I sat one spring night in a chapel where I had been placed in the first pew. It was decorated with lovely flowers and there was a certain gaiety about it that I felt didn't exactly belong there. But this chapel had to serve two purposes: for worship and for social events. I could visualize it on a Sunday morning with an altar and a cross, but now the velvet curtains were drawn concealing scuffing, whispering figures on the big platform. There was to be a play that night and I was the honored guest.

This could have been the prelude to any gay evening, I was thinking as I sat there, an evening of fun where a group of ladies were meeting to enjoy the artists and the refreshments that awaited them after the performance. Yes, the excitement was there, the flowers, the atmosphere created by the girl appointed to stand guard by the velvet curtains and the distinguished gray-haired lady who skillfully played the organ. It could have been all fun and laughter, with an author flown in from a distant place to see her own creation, a chapter from a book she had written, acted out by amateurs who had a knack for that sort of thing.

It was even hard for me to remember that whatever name had been given the place, it was still a reformatory and these women were serving time for crimes they had committed.

I had arrived early in plenty of time to observe and to think. In my heart there were mixed emotions, but primarily gratitude to those dear women who liked my book, PAPA's WIFE, so well that they had chosen to dramatize a chapter. And I rejoiced for the friend who had given them the book and her time to help with the work of the play, and who had accompanied me to the chapel. And I had only praise for the lovely warden, a wonderful woman with a vision of transforming this institution into a warm, livable place for those who had erred. Already the walls had been changed from a drab gray to pastels, each cell painted in light, sunny shades. They were orderly, comfortable rooms where a person could think and hope to make restitution if she were willing to seek a higher aim in life. I was more excited than I had ever been before, because this was the first time I would see my own creation through someone else's eyes, real and moving. Despite all this, I could not erase the sadness deep, deep within me. Why did young girls and women have to go wrong, when God had so generously given the same power to all—the strength to endure in time of temptation? But I ought not think of that sad part. I was here to enjoy a play and I would, for if I made up my mind to do it, I could—even if it was in a prison.

Everything went off to perfection! What skill and talent was wasting away within those walls! I was carried away with the warmth and humor of my own story, which I found really worth listening to.

There were also other talented women who performed. A chorus sang many beautiful selections and a very young girl, with a tiny, childlike, angelic face, sang. At the end of the performance, a gorgeous corsage was presented to me by the chairman of the play with words that warmed my heart. I would commit them to the pages of my memory and in the future years as I looked back, I would turn those pages one by one and relive those memories again and again.

When it came my turn to speak, I arose with a big lump in my throat and eyes burning from unshed tears. My heart pounded fast and hard as I faced my audience, that sea of faces, young and old, different features and expressions, but eyes all the same as though the light had been blown out of them. Although their lips smiled, their eyes didn't change. I had chosen for my topic: To Dare To Dream. I spoke without notes; in fact, I let my mind rest and my heart did the talking. I could see that my words touched them for now and then a tear rolled down a worn cheek or the stony face of a young girl. And as I talked on and on, it seemed as though some of the faces challenged me. It was as though they were saying:

"It's all right for you to talk. You have had a life sheltered with love and happiness. What did we have? If you only could take a peek into our pasts, perhaps you would not have the nerve to stand there, telling us these things. Life was against us from the beginning, but you would not understand. Only we understand why we are here, locked up so as not to hurt the outside world."

It was hard for me to talk. I felt there was so little I could say. I did not want to say another word, but rather to take them all in my arms and make them understand that I cared and, more than I, God cared and loved them all.

During the social hour that followed, I had a chance to talk to some of them. Their curfew had been extended that night to eleven o'clock. Many of the women thanked me for my book and for my talk. There was one young girl who asked me if I would give her a few moments; there was something she wanted to talk over with me. We sat down on a bench away from the rest.

"I'll be out of here in a few days," she said slowly. "I think that God must have sent you to give that talk especially for me. I have always wanted to be a singer. I know I have a good voice, but do you think there would be a chance for me after having served time?"

"I am sure there would!" I answered, hoping with all my heart the world would be kind to her.

"I think now I would dare to dream," she went on, "if only I could forget my bitterness against the woman who took away my happiness. You see, I wanted to kill her, but I didn't get very far. I was in once before and when I was free, I went for her again. Hate does that! You can't help yourself."

"It is like a hurricane," I said. "It tears down and destroys, stopping at nothing until the calm finally comes. And then what a pity to look at all that destruction, done just in a few moments."

"You're right; you can't stop hating once you start."

"Would you care to tell me your story?" I ventured.

"Yes, I want to. I know it will help to talk about it.

I need advice. You see, I loved a man, not knowing he was already married. But even if I had known, I don't think it would have made any difference. I came from a broken home. All I can remember is cursing and swearing and parents stumbling around too drunk to walk. I had my dreams when I was a little girl. I used to love to sing my doll to sleep. But I wished my mother wouldn't cry so much and that my stepfather wouldn't hit her. I began to do the wrong thing early. No one seemed to care what I did or with whom I went out, or when I came in. Then I met this man and fell in love, really in love. My whole world changed. I wanted a happy home for him with children who laughed and sang and were not afraid of their father. I was very young when I left the place I had called home. We rented a small room in the dingy part of town. We were never married. He told me that marriage was just a paper, but people who loved each other were married in their hearts before God and that was all that counted. And we were happy. Oh, we had so little and some days he didn't come home to me; sometimes he was gone for a week at a time, but I knew he always would come back and when he returned and I was in his arms, I forgave him whatever it was that had kept him away so long. I was going to have a baby. It was frightening, but he assured me all would be well. But when my time came, he was gone again, I couldn't find him, I didn't know where to turn. I was sent to a home for unmarried mothers. He never came to me. But there was the baby, so little—tiny as a doll. I held her in my arms and I loved her as much as any mother could love her child. But they told me I had to prove I could support her before I could have her and until then she had to be a state child."

She stopped and wiped the tears from her eyes.

"It was too much of a sorrow. I couldn't bear it," she said, and now her voice was under control. "I never have seen my baby since. And now, after being locked up twice, I probably never will. The authorities saw to it that I got a job and I moved home with mother again. I had only one thought in mind and that was to find him. I wanted to hear in his own words why he had left me. I found him all right. I found more than him. I found that he was married and had a family living in the better part of town. I couldn't hate him, but I hated the one that was his wife with all the hate my young heart could hold. One night I went there. She opened the door, and I went for her face. I was pretty rough. He stopped me and called the police. He claimed he didn't know me. They put me away for a while. I couldn't wait to get out so I could finish her. I tried again, but failed completely and I only got a longer sentence. But it is up now. I had planned to . . . well . . . your talk has changed that. For the first time I realize I have only hurt myself and my own future. I'll never come back here again. I want to do what is right. I want to be a great singer! Perhaps someday I can have my child? Oh, do you think I can dream my dream high enough?"

"I know you can! God will help you. I shall pray that you will meet wonderful people who will help you. Someday you will look back on these years as only a bad dream. Just let go of your bitterness and resentment, try to overcome the evil with good."

"Thank you," she whispered, tears gleaming in her eyes and a smile on her lips.

And I have prayed for this young girl and I know wherever she is my prayers will follow her. Perhaps I shall never know the outcome of her life, but God will know. For doesn't He leave the ninety-and-nine to seek that lost little lamb? She, too, was a lost little lamb. Long after that visit, I could still see her eager face, her eyes filling, her expression becoming bitter and changing again. I prayed that in some way I really had helped her to find herself. Even if it was just to give her courage to dare to dream, it would be worth all my prayers.

It took me a long time to feel peaceful again after that visit. And I long remembered that spring night. God could change that girl's life and other unhappy lives, too, making them shine with joy and beauty from within. All I could do was to leave it with God. For God can make life beautiful!

When I think of beauty, my mind strays to a lovely big home on a mountaintop in the State of Vermont. I was invited to stay here as an overnight guest during one of my trips. There lived a man who had fallen in love with that mountain many years before. He had often taken rides in his car up those hills and a sadness had always filled his heart when he saw the tumbled-down old farmhouse erected there. The people who lived in it seemed to have no eye for beauty. Year after year, the farm looked sadder and sadder. One day he noticed that the people had moved out and there was a "For Sale" sign on it. The farm had become an empty shell—a house with nobody in it.

Most of the man's friends thought he had lost his mind when one day he sold his comfortable modern home in the city and purchased the old house. But they soon discovered they were wrong. He had had a vision of what that farmhouse could become. It took plenty of hard work by his whole family, as things were torn down, new lumber replacing the old. For a long, long time their labor was tedious and they had to wait for things they could not afford until they had money to purchase them. But eventually the transformation had taken place, his vision had come true and there stood a stately mansion with a view so breath-taking that eyes could not feast on it long enough.

He had sold his comfortable modern home and paid a sum of money for this place. But the things he valued most could never have been bought. Those things had been a gift from God, thrown in as extras. There were the hills, the valley and snow-covered mountain peaks as far as the eye could see. He had made this transformation with a house, but I couldn't help thinking how many times God had done the same thing with a human being. The world may put little value on a certain life, but God sees its potential if only He has a chance to make it over.

I went to bed early the night of my visit. The mountain air had made me so sleepy that I couldn't keep my eyes open. My friends graciously excused me and it took me only a moment to fall asleep. It must have been about two o'clock in the morning when I awakened as if a hand had touched my shoulder. I sat up. The room was white with moonlight. I slid out of bed and walked to the big window facing the mountains and stood there spellbound. I don't think in all my life I had ever seen anything so breath-takingly beautiful as the countryside I gazed upon. The mountains and hills were like black silhouettes against the star-studded sky. A round gold moon hung over the highest mountain peak, and below, far below, lay a sleeping village. This world looked so peaceful and contented. My heart, it seemed, couldn't hold such beauty by itself. I wanted so to awaken the household, but one just doesn't do that. Somehow, I had to be content with hugging all that beauty to my own heart, knowing that in the morning I would have to travel on. These lucky people! Because of a man with a vision, they feasted on this view night and day.

I went back to bed, but sleep would not come. My heart was suddenly sad because I thought how ungrateful mankind was to God who had created this beautiful world. It was as though I longed to make amends, as I whispered:

Father God, I don't know just how to thank you in behalf of all the world for all the things You have given us. Forgive us when we forget You so easily. The tenderness with which You have planted trees and bushes and flowers, the magnificence of your mountains and forests, birds and all wild life that lives and moves there, Your bubbling brooks, blue lakes, and great oceans, for these I thank You. And I thank You for the smallest flowers and the softest moon beam and most of all, because You are a loving Father.

And then it came to me what a blessing it was that I could see beauty and feel it in my heart. So many had eyes, but they couldn't see, and their hearts had no room to tuck in little beauties. And I wondered if this night, so significant in its splendor, would always be retained in my mind like the other things that had etched themselves there.

There seemed to be three special occasions that have gone with me always through my life here on earth and that have become guides for my reasoning.

The first memory was from my early childhood. I was in Sweden and only three years old, standing on the deck of the ship. The family must have been on a trip, although I cannot remember anything about it. But I can feel myself standing there on the deck floor, feeling very small. In my hand I held a toy, a little milk pail. It was shiny and new and my heart thrilled that it was mine. I can remember hands lifting me up on to the rail so I could see the ocean. I leaned over and looked far, far down and I saw the big blue-green waves. The sight of those great waves frightened me and I let go of my toy and watched it fall into that wet grave, sink and disappear. With it went my heart. I sorrowed for days over my loss. And strangely enough, to think about it now, still brings pain to my heart. Was the ocean as deep as a sorrowing heart? Was that the lesson I had to learn? Otherwise, why didn't I ever forget it? And even now when sorrow comes, I am still that little girl, seeing that toy disappear from my sight. Perhaps it gave me a better understanding of suffering and helped my heart to know how much there is to bear in the world.

There was a different night that found me, a teen-ager, waiting for the man to whom I had pledged my heart. It was a crisp fall night, with the scent of burning leaves filling the air. The dark velvety sky was pinpricked with a million glittering stars. And I remember looking up into that firmament and wondering how far it was up to those stars. Even if I could have measured the distance, I thought, it would be too high to count. At that moment I was completely happy because my love was just as great as that unmeasured distance. It could never be measured, it was too great to count. I knew then that many times during the numerous tomorrows we would spend together as husband and wife, when disappointments would come or we would be on the outs with each other, that moment under the stars would come back to me. And it has. I knew then that my love was great enough to get over whatever obstacles might stand in our way and a new wonder at the heights of love filled my heart anew.

Then there was the third time: I had been through a serious operation and for a few days had been wavering between holding on or letting go completely. I had been unconscious for days and had no memory of my family sitting beside my bed. But as my mind began to clear, I seemed to remember one thing from my long siege. I knew my husband had been there beside me. Twice someone had touched my nose lightly, a particular caress which only he used. And in my fight for life, that slight touch had given me the will to live. It was the security of love, as broad as the distance from east to west. Since that time, if ever I question the strength of love, I feel again that touch and a warm wave of security floods my heart.

Those memories, too, are blessings from God. Often we wander away from His love, but there must always be a return home, because His love is inescapable and stronger than any human love. And He, also, has His special ways to make us remember the little things that He has planted in our hearts to keep us from ever separating ourselves from that love.

I would like very much to believe that for one moment this world would change, that for a short space of time everyone in this whole universe would join in a prayer that would envelop the whole earth like a cloak. I would like to visualize each person, from the smallest baby to the most aged oldster, lifting his heart in complete honesty to his Lord. There would be a hush in prisons and institutions as a smile came to the lips of strong men hardened by hate and crime because God's love came into their hearts. There would be a light in the eyes of the mentally ill and a stillness would linger over sickbeds and hospitals as hope and peace replaced the sting of pain in tortured bodies. Little children would laugh, free from fear and hurt, as husbands and wives in that instant renewed their vows to each other. I can see it now, king and peasant, president and general, bishop, minister and priest, and all faiths united. For just one moment there would be no division, no labor problems, no jealousy, no hate. Even in nature, trees, bushes, flowers and plants, animals and birds would offer up their silent tribute of praise to their Creator. And again there would be an Eden, a paradise . . . God's kingdom on earth.

But although a universal prayer offered simultaneously by the whole world cannot be, we who do believe can build our own worlds within our own hearts and, as His servants, we can usher others into that moment of prayer. And because of the good that can shine forth from our world within a world, love can overcome some of the hate. Evil can be covered by the power of good, with peace filling the heart instead of tension. We can plant happiness wherever we go and sorrow can disappear as trust supersedes suspicion. . . . It would take so little on the part of each of us to change so much and make it right.

And I and my friend, the imagination, would still like to believe that we could build a big bonfire of all resentments, mistrust, evil thinking and worries, a fire that would burn high and long, turning them all into ashes. And after the fire had died away, we who desire to serve God would never let anything but good thoughts enter in. What a glorious world for us to live in—God's world! It would be a world ruled by love, a love that could drive away all fear.

How seldom we realize that we are just guests in this world and that our bodies are but the earthly homes of our souls, which we stay in only a number of years called "time." But this I know, that this person within, the real me, when I have moved out of my earthly dwelling, will move into a new world, a new dimension, a higher level. And I will step upward . . . upward until I am once again united with my Creator.

Chapter Seven

Someone asked me one day just recently, "Does God always answer your prayers? Is there such a thing as an unanswered prayer?"

I didn't speak at once. To me, there are no unanswered prayers. Although it might not seem so to many people, God always answers a true prayer, a prayer that comes from a humble heart, seeking for a solution. Perhaps people do not understand that because God answers in His way and sometimes it is not to our liking. A prayer must always be ended, "Thy will, not mine, oh Lord."

I have written in this book about the many, many prayers God has answered in a tangible way, a way that I could see with my eyes and sometimes touch with my hands. They have been wonderful to experience, these answers, because they have made my heart sing and my faith grow in such a way that it has become a "knowing" faith that can now trust without seeing.

When I think of the many seemingly unanswered prayers, I think of a lady I met on one of my long speaking tours. I was far from home and, being a home-loving person, hotels are to me very dismal places in which to stay. When a program chairman realizes this and takes a special interest in seeing that I share a bit of her company, it makes me doubly joyful.

I had sensed that this fine woman was in need of friendship. She told me that she belonged to a small prayer group in her church and that she was a hard worker among the young people. But she had a great problem that was almost breaking her heart. We had had lunch and dinner and spent the evening together and were walking back to my hotel, when she opened up her heart to me.

As she talked, I glanced down at her eager face. She was a tiny person with almost childlike features. It was a lovely face that had succeeded in hiding the tears and heartache that would have shown had she not have been such a clever actress.

"Perhaps you have wondered why I haven't invited you to my home to share this time before your train?" she said. "Well, I will tell you because I have a feeling you can help me. You see, we live on the wrong side of the tracks. My husband could have been a successful businessman with money, position and a happy disposition, but he refuses to progress with his time or his job of the future; and today he is exactly where he was the day I married him. Once I got him, in a weak moment, to buy a lot in one of the better sections of town. The value of that lot has more than doubled during the years. But instead of building our lovely home on it, he is going to sell it. The only thing that has kept him from doing it is the thought that soon the prices will be even higher and he will make more money on it. You know, for years I have been praying and dreaming that I would live on that spot. I have driven up to it at night, stopped and visualized our home standing there. My faith has been so strong and my hope so great that now, when I see it about to crumble to ashes, I can hardly bear it. I know I shall always live where we live now if I stay on with him and that my dreams will fade away one after another."

"I wish I could help you," I said softly. "I wish I

knew a way, but all I can say is that I will pray that God will make your dreams come true."

"Thank you." She smiled through her tears. "I shall treasure that thought and I shall know that I am not alone as I pray, but that you will join yours with mine."

"And you must stop fretting about it, my dear. Try not to think hostile thoughts toward this man who is your husband. You must lift him up and see him as the man he ought to be."

"I know the method, the love way, the Christ way. I will try as long as I have strength to go on. But it isn't just the new house. It's also that he hinders me from taking civic positions that I could hold if my address were different."

"Yes, but you can work in your church and hold positions there, high or low."

"That's true. I have my church as my field, but in clubs or any place of importance in the community, I'm licked."

She told me many other things about her husband. They poured forth like liquid from a bottle that has just popped its cork, having been too full too long. And I could see that man so clearly, a man from an old European stock, a stubborn man who refused to budge even one inch, who scoffed at progress and was antisocial. What a life for this darling little lady to live! She should have been sparkling with joy and radiance. She was as brilliant as she was pretty, but she had that longing in her eyes to live life, to give and take like other women, and to follow the pattern indicated by talents God had given her. She really did carry many heavy burdens and I promised I would pray that God would change things for her. We prayed before I left and as I held her small hand, it clutched mine as a drowning person's would. Tears rolled down her cheeks as I heard her pray:

"Dear God, I want all these things, but I am willing to wait until your time comes. I desire to be a great light shining for you in my community. You have given me so many talents, but if your will for me is to be a small light on a back porch, I shall be just that until you let me shine in a greater way."

She said many more things in her wonderful prayer, which was so humble and sweet that I almost expected God to send an angel down to straighten out her life right then and there. But the answer has still not come, and we have been praying for years now.

You wonder why, I do, too. But I know that God is answering in His own wonderful way and someday we will see that answer. In the meantime she writes me several times a year. And when her letters come, I glance down at the address and my heart sinks a little to see that it is still the same. Why doesn't God answer? But I have learned never to question God. His ways are wise. He knows why, and His love never fails her. Her life has been more radiant since that night we talked. As she writes in one of her dear letters:

I have come very close to God these last years. I can now take this life and make the best of it. I have been working on coming closer to this strange man I married. There is a loneliness in his self-willed heart. I am praying now that he will open it and let me fill it with love.

The material things don't matter as much if only he would place his hand in God's and let Him fill his life with joy. . . .

And I say to myself, "Isn't that an answer? Isn't it like that crippled old man's prayer so long ago?" God is making a beautiful vessel to serve Him. She is serving even now as a great light just where she is and someday she will help her husband to find God's love. But to the world, that is not an answered prayer— only to those who can pray again and again: "Not my will, Lord, but thine."

I have come in contact with many cases like that one, and I haven't seen the closing chapters of them yet. I need only to look back on my own writing career to trace God's way. As I myself waited many years and thought my prayers were lost, God was fulfilling them in the most magnificent way which I would never have dared to dream of.

I have talked to Mama about unanswered prayer and what she thinks about it. And, as always, she makes me see it so clearly.

"It is easy to understand," she says in her soft voice, "if we think of our own children. Can we grant them anything they wish for? Don't we know that sometimes they ask us for things that would harm them? We really answer them the right way—we refuse to give them what they ask."

Yes, God, in His wonderful love and desire to grant us what we ask, gives His angels orders to sort out our prayers. Some prayers are not prayers at all, but only the selfish desire to fulfill a longing in a person's heart to possess certain things. A thing that God, in His wisdom knows would not be for our own good.

A true prayer should be a giving prayer. Whatever we ask for should help us to grow closer to our Creator, and we should pray, not just for things to be given to us, but also to our fellow men.

But this thought also comes to me often: when we receive, we must also give out in turn to others. Such giving is like an artesian well: the more we give, the more is given to us so that we may give again.

"Give and it shall be given unto you," said the Master. *Giving* is also a form of prayer. Many are the gifts we should ask God for—especially the opportunity to be useful during our earthly journey, and for *the spirit of giving*, which is one of the greatest of the gifts.

Mama has that gift and she uses it in everyday living. It has always amazed me, this love that Mama possesses to give out. And because of it she will never lack things because the Master has said: "As ye measure to others, so shall it be measured unto you."

Mama lives on a very small monthly income, but she gives as though there always was an abundance to take from. First of all, she gave her own life to God, promising to do His will. When she married a minister, she gave to him her very best; nothing was too hard, his work became her work. As the children came, one by one, she gave all eight of us to God.

"They are yours, Father," she said. "You have just loaned them to me. Help me never to stand in the way so that Your will can be done in their lives."

And I remember many times in the days of my childhood, when strangers dropped in at the parsonage as we were about to sit down to a meal. How willingly she shared what there was! And I am sure God stretched the food because there was always enough for all.

One day recently Mama was a little low on funds. She had only two dollars in her billfold and still a half a week to go before more would come. She was on an errand down in Miami, Florida, where she lives, when on impulse she decided to dine in the big ten-cent store around the corner. It would be economical, she decided, as she could eat a bowl of soup for a quarter and so save on her slim budget. As she sat down at the counter, a lady sat down beside her. She looked very gloomy and downhearted and all the warmth of Mama's soul went out to give her some joy.

"I was just about to have dinner," said Mama lightly. "Why don't you be my guest and we can eat together?"

The lady was more than willing to accept the invitation, and Mama thought it would be good for her to have a big bowl of soup, too. But instead of soup her newfound friend ordered a big dinner that cost Mama $1.65. Mama never regretted it.

"She was very hungry," she said. "I was so glad to share with her."

And the next day, when Mama opened her mail, there was a five-dollar bill in a letter. She wasn't a bit surprised.

"My wonderful God is like that," she beamed. "He never lets me do anything for Him but right away He sends it back to me . . . and always, always He gives me more than I gave Him."

And she goes on her mission tours, giving a little plant here and a basket of fruit to someone else, but most of all, in words and prayer, she shares her precious faith in God.

At times I know Mama's giving became a real sacrifice. I am thinking now of one certain time when I know Mama gave so it hurt. After Papa had left us, Mama drove a little Ford that was somehow a part of her. She loved to take off for long trips and she traveled far and wide. We children never considered Mama a good driver, and we thought perhaps it was because she had been too old when she learned to drive and never really got the knack of it. Or it might be that she had her unique way of living. Mama never liked to be tied down to rules. But despite this fact, Mama never lacked passengers. It is true that people sometimes sat on the edge of the seat when she decided to step on the gas, but they always knew the ride would end well. As one old lady confided to me: "The way she goes about it, sometimes you wonder what is going to happen . . . and you know she just can't make it . . . but, you see, we all know that God drives that car and it is the safest place to ride in."

Many things we still laugh about as we remember

the days when Mama drove her Ford. She did not believe in stop signs.

"Why should one stop," she sighed, "when not a soul is coming? Just a waste of gas."

Once she parked her car outside a drugstore, under a big sign that warned: ABSOLUTELY NO PARKING AT ANY TIME. But Mama had looked around and calmly parked right under the sign. She proceeded into the store and when she returned, there was an officer of the law waiting for her.

"Lady, can't you read?" he asked curtly.

"Of course I can read, officer," Mama smiled, looking rather surprised at such an accusation.

"Then why did you park your car here?" the policeman snapped, taking out his pad and pencil. "It warns clearly enough, no parking at any time."

Mama smiled her sunniest smile and she patted him lightly on the shoulder.

"I'll tell you why," she said almost in a whisper. "I was in a hurry and I looked around and there just wasn't another place to park. Now will you please run along so I can get home with this medicine?"

She stepped into the car . . . still smiling and waving as she drove off. The police officer just stood there staring after her. He shook his head slowly and put his unused pad back in his pocket, but there was a smile playing on his lips as he walked off and he looked like a happy man.

When the time came that one of Mama's daughters was going to be married to a minister, her joy knew no bounds. There was a strange twinkle in her eye. She had a surprise wedding gift for them; it was so small, she hinted she could keep it in her pocket. We were all curious as to what it was and tried to pry it out of her, but she would tell no one. It was her big secret. And when the day came that she presented her gift —a small box carefully wrapped with all the frills appropriate for a wedding gift—we hardly could believe it. It was a small key. The key to Mama's

Ford. How could she do it? we wondered. That car meant everything to her. But she explained that she really didn't need it. She used it only for her own pleasure, while the young man who was to become her son-in-law had no car and perhaps could not afford one for years. It would be selfish of her to drive around while he might need to reach the sick or the bereaved quickly. . . . So that was the gift she gave.

The car was shined and polished when the newlyweds drove off. Mama's eyes had a strange shine to them, too, but we could not detect whether a tear gleamed in them as she saw her beloved Ford make the turn at the bend of the road.

One day I sat down to note on paper how much Mama had given to others during a month's time. I didn't get very far, for I soon discovered she had given much more than her income, but still she had money left over. Who can understand the mystery of such giving? But that too is part of Mama's way.

I do sincerely pray that someday I will possess her gift. That I also will give, knowing that giving to others, prompted by love, is sometimes a greater prayer than mere uttered words.

Who on this earth can understand the magic of prayer? Volumes of books have been written on it, but the secret of it is still in the souls of men. Many times I have stood perplexed when great Christians have suffered difficulties and gone through deep waters while prayers from scores of people have gone up for them—and still seemingly no answer. We have to learn then to say with Paul:

My grace is sufficient for thee: for my strength is made perfect in weakness.

Many things in the prayer world are happening in silence known only to individuals who hug the mystery and glory of it to their own hearts. But God knows all things and to trust Him in all His ways

Chapter Eight

To some people a lecturer seems to live a very glamorous life. They picture me as traveling in style from one great city to another, always being honored and surrounded by admiring people. It is true in many ways; meeting people and seeing new places is a pleasure, but it involves a lot more than happy traveling. Sometimes there are lonely days and nights in hotel rooms far from home; there are planes that are grounded when there is a fog, trains that are hours late, or a drive in the car through a storm, along icy roads or in deep snow. But the greatest joy I have found on my many, many miles of traveling is the knowledge that wherever I am God is with me. There is no lonely place when I can pray. There is no place so dangerous that His hand cannot protect me and when I am back safe and sound in my dear home, I am filled with joy and gratitude because I can tell the story again: He was with me in a special way.

At the beginning of 1959 as I glanced through my engagement book and remembered I was to go on a speaking tour in the Middle West in the spring, I had a strange premonition that I should not take this trip. I am a sensitive person and premonitions have very often proved to be a true warning against a catastrophe. So, acting on an impulse, I sat down to cancel these engagements, only to realize that engagements are not canceled that easily as there are such things as contracts involved. I soon concluded that I must take this trip regardless of my feelings.

As the day for my departure drew near and I checked the airlines for passage, I had again that same strong feeling—this time that I should not fly. Free to follow my own judgment, I gave up the thought of flying and checked on train schedules only to find out that every train I would have to take would bring me to a strange city and in the very early morning hours. One thing I detest is arriving as a stranger in a city when it is asleep, so I canceled out the thought of trains and fell back on driving my own car.

My husband objected vigorously. "What about snowstorms?" he asked anxiously. "This is March and sometimes we even have big storms in the month of April."

"Well if I get stuck, I get stuck," I said nonchalantly, but I later agreed it would be a good thing for me to have a companion, such as my secretary, to share that long drive, someone to talk to on the long miles that had to be traveled.

A friend of mine, a pleasant person and a good driver, said she would be happy to travel with me, so my mind was at ease as I began to pack for the trip.

The Middle West experienced one of their worst snowstorms in many decades the week before we left. How happy I was that it had been the week before. Now surely we would have nice weather, because a storm like that does not repeat itself very often. But as it was we started off in a New England snowstorm, one that had blown up after a spell of warm spring weather. As we drove on and the miles accumulated behind us, we found the roads free from snow and it seemed as though driving had after all been the right choice.

We had been on the road two days when we

learned from our radio that snow was racing around us on both sides. Toward the south and north, within thirty or forty miles there were big snowstorms, but my heart was light. I had left this trip in God's care and surely we would be protected. The sun would shine and the roads would be good and all would work out even better than we could have expected.

I was thinking how wonderfully I had always been protected on my long automobile travelings. Ever since that time when my car left the icy road, nothing had happened that could be termed dangerous. Oh, there had been that flat tire, but just once. And having a flat tire come your way only once, when you have been going on lecture trips for six years is not too bad. It had been a little frightening when it had happened, of course. It had been in Connecticut late one night, past midnight. I had been traveling through woodland for miles and miles, on my way from a lecture, when suddenly the car swirled and my heart sank. "Oh! no," I said out loud, "it can't be!" But it was a flat tire and I, not knowing how to change it, had to drive along at a snail's pace, hoping that I would come to some house, some place, where light would be shining. After ten miles more of driving with tense nerves and a ruined front tire, I saw a light . . . a bright, shining light. I stopped and discovered that it came from a tavern. I didn't dare to go inside, so I sat by the roadside waiting. After a while a man came out and I called to him:

"What does a gal do when she is stuck with a flat tire in the middle of the night and doesn't know how to change it?"

He didn't even look my way, but he answered in a very indifferent voice, "She is out of luck, I would say, for all the garages are closed."

My heart prayed desperately. I was a little afraid. Here I was on a lonely country road, in a car I couldn't go on with, talking to a man who was very unsteady on his legs, outside a tavern filled with many souls like him. I had to have help and one thing my mind must be sure of was God would never fail me.

"Listen," I almost shouted, "you don't think there would be a couple of gentlemen who would care to help a lady in distress?"

He started back to the tavern. "I will find out," he called back.

A moment later he came out accompanied by two other men. They were on the glad side, but they were very helpful and kind and changed the tire very quickly. I offered up my thankfulness to my heavenly Father as I handed each one my book "PAPA'S WIFE."

"I am an author," I explained, thanking them. "Take my book as a souvenir. I hope you will read about how my Mama always got herself out of trouble. I feel very much like her tonight."

When we reached Joliet, Illinois, we were told the forecast had been for four inches of snow, but the weather had changed its mind and no snow had appeared. Those words sounded good to me and it really seemed as though this trip would be free from trouble after all.

Then in Moline, Illinois, it happened. I had spoken to a women's club group on a Saturday afternoon and Sunday morning we would have to start for a city three hundred miles away, located in the northern part of Wisconsin. As we were retiring for the night, we listened to the weather forecast for the following day and my heart stood still. There was a prediction that the big snowstorm of the week before would repeat itself. On top of that there would be winds up to tornado force, and if that were not enough, there would also be thunder and lightning.

"What are we to do?" asked my companion. "We certainly cannot start out in weather like that."

"We have to go," I said firmly. "When you are scheduled to speak at a club, it does not matter what the weather is, you have to get there, that's all."

We left it there. I know my friend was not very happy. Evidently she had thought it would be glamorous to travel with a lecturing author and it had been fun until now. But she would know very soon that this kind of life is not always easy.

As I knelt to pray that night, I talked things over with my heavenly Father. He had changed the weather before. Perhaps through His love and care there would be another forecast for better weather in the morning. With that thought in mind I went to sleep, only to be awakened about three by a terrific thunder crash. I rushed from my bed and looked out from the sixth-story hotel window. The wind was blowing with such a might that signs and everything that could be pried loose were blowing about on the streets. It seemed that the wind would crash through the windows any moment, and it was snowing—snowing hard and drifting because of the strong winds. I was glad my friend was sleeping. As it was, I couldn't believe my eyes.

"Oh, God" [I whispered, disappointed and with a terrible let-down feeling] "how could you let it happen? You know I asked you not to let it snow. I have to go! Don't I? I tried so hard to get out of it, but I was so sure You would pave the way for me, that You would answer my prayer as You have done before. Now what shall we do?"

It did not occur to me that I was scolding God as I stood there looking out on the drama the wind and snow played. It was only moments later that I became penitent. Who was I to talk like that to God? Shouldn't His promise to be with me until the end of the world be enough for me? He had not promised that my way would be easy, but He had promised that wherever I was, He would be near. I knelt to pray for forgiveness for my arrogance and my heart was calm once more. I would start out with my hand in God's, trusting Him through the storm.

It was a little hard to convince my friend that starting out would be wise. The radio had been blaring about the destruction the snowstorm had brought. Planes were grounded and trains were stuck in mountains of snow. My premonition had been right after all. If I had traveled by either of those means of transportation, I surely would have been stranded. Everything was canceled because of the snow—church services and other activities; even some of the newspapers were not being delivered. Roads were blocked and most of them closed. State police warned that only those facing some emergency should drive as the roads were more than icy—they were hazardous. But with three hundred miles ahead of us, we had at least to start out.

The garage man at the filling station shook his head as he dug out my car. He didn't say anything, but I know he wondered if I was in my right mind even to think of starting out on a day like this. We ate a hearty breakfast before we checked out of the hotel. Who knew when we would eat next? It was nine A.M. as we drove into Davenport, Iowa. It was really tough to drive, but we moved forward anyway, and if we only could keep going, the trip would take time, but we would make it.

The miles do not pile up very fast when you drive fifteen . . . ten . . . five miles an hour. The wind whipped the snow in a wild fury and it surely had a wide playground over those miles and miles of Iowa field land. The world turned into a whirling, crazy merry-go-round. Sometimes we couldn't see the road and then we had to stop because the windows were covered with white, glistening snow. It became almost unbearable, all that whiteness; it affected the eyeballs till they ached like a toothache, there was no end to it. The roads were deserted, no life anywhere. It seemed as though my car was the only thing moving in this whole white world. All eating places were closed so we could not reinforce ourselves with so much as a cup of hot coffee. Once we found a gas station open and although we had plenty of gas, we filled the tank. It was that feeling: one never knows when one will see an open gas station again.

How glad I was that I was not alone. My friend was a good sport. She never complained. She no longer seemed the least big apprehensive. How many ladies, I was thinking, would have been scared to death riding in a car on this day. I was lucky she was the one who had had enough faith in me to take this long trip. We talked, we sang, we tried to recall amusing incidents to tell each other—anything to make the time go faster.

"My family will be worried about me when they read in the newspapers how bad the storm is out here," she said once.

"Mine never worry about me," I stated calmly. "My husband claims that if I got stranded on top of a high lonely mountain, someone would suddenly appear and bring me down safely."

"But this is a terrific storm," she insisted.

"I know," I answered, thinking longingly of home. "It could be that perhaps even my family are worried this time."

We had gone a little over fifty miles by that time. It was two o'clock in the afternoon. Only fifty miles since nine o'clock that morning!

Presently we saw ahead of us something that looked like cars—a long, long line of them all standing still. Could this be the end of our trip?

We soon learned that there was a snowplow ahead. The road had been cleared on one side only. How fortunate we were that it was our side! We moved slowly behind the plow. Like a funeral procession, evenly, at snail pace. At two thirty P.M. we arrived in the little town of Zwingle, Iowa. Here the plow stopped and we were informed that that was as far as we could go; from now on our destiny depended on a plow from Dubuque County and very likely it would be a long, long time before it came through.

There were thirty cars sitting in a long row like white ducks. It was a closed highway ahead of us and the snow was drifting higher and higher. It was long past lunchtime. We had not eaten since morning. This town had no restaurant open because it was Sunday. There was no place for tourists!

As the plow turned around to plow the other side of the road I, on impulse, pulled out and turned around, too.

"Are you going back?" asked my companion. "What in the world would be the sense of going back?"

"I don't know why I turned back," I confessed. "You must get used to me. I do things . . . I don't know why, sometimes."

The plow had stopped. I passed it and up the road a bit I stopped beside a man who was out shoveling snow.

"Tell me, is there a Protestant minister in this town?" I heard myself ask.

"Sure thing," he laughed. "You are parked by the parsonage."

"What do you want the minister for?" asked my friend.

"You wait and see," said I. Suddenly a bright idea had come to my mind.

I went back and asked the plow men to clear a little place beside the road so I could park my car safely. Then, leaving my friend in the car, I stepped kneedeep into the drifts to reach the parsonage door. I made it, looking like a snow-man myself, but I rang the bell and the door opened and I stood face to face with a friendly minister. In a few moments I had told him our predicament and he had invited me and my friend into the cozy living room.

"I am a minister's daughter," I laughed. "That is why I am bold enough to come in like this. You see parsonages to me are the friendliest places in the world."

"Of course," he said warmly. "That is what we are here for. I want you to feel at home and stay as long as you need to."

His wife came into the room having been awakened from her Sunday-afternoon nap. She was as kindly as her husband.

"I believe God had His hand in this," she said. "You see we always have a big Sunday dinner a little after noon on Sundays, but for some strange reason I couldn't seem to get started to cook it today. Now I know why. We were to have guests! We'll love sharing our dinner with you two snowbound travelers."

So we had a tasty chicken dinner in the lovely parsonage while outside the wind blew and the drifting continued. We talked and rested and the time went by. At ten o'clock that night the plow from Dubuque had still not come through. We learned later that it didn't come until much later—in the early morning hours. The cars we had come in with were still sitting there. My heart ached for them, but it was also running over in gratitude to my Heavenly Father. He always looked out for me . . . always. . . . How could I ever love Him enough for all He did for me? Yes, right here on the snowy fields of Iowa, His love surrounded me. . . . He had cared for me in a way that I would never forget and He had given us shelter in the storm.

We spent the night in the parsonage. After a good sleep and a fine breakfast we started off early the next morning. The plow had been through by then. The sun was shining and the wind had died down. It was a beautiful, beautiful world and though the road was icy in spots and plowed only on one side in many places, we reached our destination in plenty of time.

It was spring weather when our fifteen-hundred-mile journey was completed and we started our long trip home, but as we came nearer and nearer our own territory, I still was thinking of that Sunday in Iowa . . . the mountains of snow . . . and the drifting of it . . . and the wind blowing over those miles and miles of Iowa farmland . . . then the lull in the storm . . . the refuge in the warm, friendly parsonage. And I whispered to myself: "Why should I ever fear when the Lord God is my God!"

Chapter Nine

People often ask me about that trip I took abroad in 1956. "Tell us a little about it," they ask. "How could you have time to visit so many countries in only three weeks?"

"Because all I wanted to do was to see a little bit of those countries. I wanted to walk on their streets and mingle with their people, get the feel of them, so to speak. My book was going to be a part of them. I was grateful that I could share my life with so many. The least I could do, when I was flying to Sweden anyway, was to pay them a little visit."

"And did you enjoy it?"

"I surely did! And it gave me many pleasant memories."

After the person has gone and I am alone, I let my thoughts wander back again to that summer when I boarded that big transatlantic plane for Sweden. I was going home to my native land after being away from it twenty-one years. The place where I was born was very dear to me and as a child I had possessed an almost passionate love for it. How often I had dreamed myself back to it in fantasy—the mountains that stood as strong guards around the little village up there in the north, the pleasant green valleys and the swift-flowing rivers. How carefree I had been, playing my games in the stately forests. It was always bitter-sweet to think about it, but now I was going home to hug it again close to my heart.

Sweden was such a tiny speck on the map, but this was the land where I was born and here I had learned to laugh and sing and pray. I had even tasted the pain of sorrow here. On long, white, romantic spring evenings I had first met love. And I had listened to the birds sing in the endless golden summer nights. Going back to see and feel it all filled my heart with such excitement there was room for nothing else.

My husband and younger daughter had come to the airport to see me off. I can still see them standing there waving as the plane lifted and we sailed into a white cloudland.

It was not my first flight . . . far from it . . . but it was my first across an ocean and I have to admit that I who trusted God to protect me on land and on sea and in everyday life, was not so sure if He could protect me while I was crossing a wide, deep ocean. I was ashamed of myself. Why couldn't I trust and be happy as I always was? It took a little while . . . a little meditation . . . and a good dose of Mama's faith before I could put the fearful thoughts away. But when I once did . . . it was for always, and as night came upon us, I could close my eyes and rest in the care of Him who never slumbers. How silly I had been to be anxious. I had acted as though I didn't have a Heavenly Father. But now I knew I should fear no more, because I loved my God so much and love driveth away all fear.

There had been so much to enjoy in Sweden and the time went much too fast. My visit with the Queen in her summer palace at the most southern peak of Sweden was the highlight of my stay there, but I had to hasten on. Sweden had not taken my first book then, but Denmark had, and England and Holland, and I would visit all those countries. A very short visit, just to stop in and say hello and good-bye.

The day I left the Queen's palace I took the ferry over *Öresund*, and went right into Copenhagen. Denmark is a quaint, gay country and I fell in love with it the moment I landed. I went to my hotel and called my publisher. They bade me welcome and were most gracious, telling me that they had planned a happy day for me; an editor would pick me up at the hotel in a half an hour and I was to go with him as he was my host for the day.

It was very exciting! I felt almost like a young girl and I hoped that the editor would be a pleasant person. When I answered the house-phone and was told that my caller had arrived and was waiting in the lobby, I hoped in my heart that he would be a very wonderful person. And he was—tall and handsome, with a pleasant smile, and a lot younger than I—but why not? It would be fun spending the day with a person like him. I was so appreciative of that publishing company, the way they had planned everything to let me, a total stranger, see all the noteworthy things in Copenhagen, the deer park where hundreds of tame deer and little fawns were running around.

"Don't pat the fawn," my host warned me, as a tiny brown Bambi-deer came up to us. "You know if you touch him, the mother will have nothing to do with him, because she will smell the touch of human flesh on her baby."

We rode in an old-fashioned wagon behind a couple of fine-looking horses. It was so much fun, laughing and talking about Denmark and its history while he pointed out houses of importance. We walked a great deal and finally took a long boatride on the blue, blue water. We had stopped to see the little mermaid sitting on the big stone, and later, in the open boat, I looked longingly to my right.

"That is Sweden," I said. "So near and still so far."

"Yes," he said. "No one remembers the wars that used to be, how they were always fighting to get land for their people. Denmark is so small, Sweden could have let them have a little chunk more."

"It was the brave Gustave Vasa that saved us from you," I laughed. "If it hadn't been for his brave actions perhaps Denmark would have had all of Sweden, and I really would have been Danish like you."

"That was a long, long time ago, and the two countries are happy and contented. Sweden's princess became our beloved Queen. All is well, there is no feud any more."

It was so pleasant to talk of history and to feel the warmth and friendship that existed. I loved Denmark! I could say it over again, but I perhaps would never have known how wonderfully kind and gracious their people could be if I had not written a book called PAPA'S WIFE, which the Danes translated.

We ended our day by going to the famous park, Tivoli, and there, in a beautiful restaurant, we had a farewell dinner.

It had been a lovely summer day but now, as so often in Scandinavia, the heavens opened and without any warning the rain poured down in buckets.

"We have to eat slowly and by the time we are through the sun will shine again," said my friend the editor.

It was cozy to sit there, warm and snug, and watch people scurry to get away from the rain. We were talking fast now; there was still so much to talk about. I told him a little of my husband and girls and he told me about his lovely wife and so our talk came to my writing.

"I always wondered," he said, "as I read your book, if there still could be a person so simple in her way of life and so naïve and uninhibited . . . could it be? Or had you written a book of that type on speculation?"

"And what do you think now?" I asked.

"Now I don't think, I know . . . YOU ARE THE BOOK!"

That was a great compliment. I told him some of my philosophy and beliefs.

"If only more people could have a faith like yours," he said, "we would have a different world today."

As we rode back to my hotel in the taxi he suddenly became very quiet. Presently he began to laugh.

"I never thought I would want to tell you this," he chuckled, "but feeling now as though we are old friends, I think it would give you a kick."

"What in the world have you held back from me?" I asked curiously.

"It is a confession! You know, when we were told in the office yesterday that one of us had to spend the day with you today, no one wanted to take you out. We didn't like the picture of you and knowing you were Baptist in religion, we thought perhaps you were very pious and there would be no fun. So we flipped a coin—and I lost."

"Poor you," I whispered, a little bit hurt, but more amused.

"Poor nothing," he said and now he looked serious, "honestly I would not have missed this day for anything."

The next morning I left Denmark for Holland. It would always be pleasant to think back to that day. I felt ten years younger; my ego had suffered a little, but that was good for me. I'll have to find a better picture if I need one for another book, I thought. . . .

It was a fine trip: the food good as always on those airlines, people pleasant to talk to, and traveling alone was an adventure, knowing no one, going to a strange land without a friend to meet me. It was all training for the new life I suddenly was living.

Holland was just the way I had pictured it. It could have stepped out of a story book. There was a big art exhibition going on and almost all hotel rooms were taken, but I managed to get one in a small second-rate hotel. I took a long walk that afternoon. I walked on

the streets of Amsterdam and mingled with the people and stood amazed at all the bicycles. Why everybody rode a bicycle! Lovers with their arms around
each other, nurses, priests, schoolchildren—all passing
in droves on bicycles. It was quaint—the docks and
windmills—Holland, the way I had dreamed about it.

In the morning, after a good night's sleep, as I
walked down the stairway to the dining room a certain aloneness faced me. I hadn't minded traveling
alone and walking alone and being by myself at night,
but this morning as I was to eat breakfast I suddenly
saw myself sitting all alone at a table. All the people
would be speaking Dutch and I would sit there like
a dumbbell. Perhaps someone would speak to me in
Dutch and I would have to tell them in English that
I was sorry I couldn't talk to them.

I was the first one in the dining room. People must
be sleeping late, I told myself . . . or were they early
and I late? I knew nothing of the customs in this
country . . . not even what time they eat breakfast. I
sat down at a small table and a maid brought me
bread and cheese and butter. Presently another lady
entered the room. She was young and pretty, walked
with light steps and headed right for my table. Now
it comes, I thought. I have to smile and make my voice
gentle when I tell her I do not understand. She spoke
to me, a long sentence. I waited until she had stopped,
then I spoke slowly, pronouncing the words as clearly
as I could.

"I don't understand . . . I speak English. . . ."

She stared at me for a moment, then she burst into
clear silvery laughter.

"But I was speaking to you in English," she said.

I was very embarrassed. I had been so sure she was
going to speak Dutch, I even heard Dutch when she
spoke English. Doesn't that prove what your mind can
do to you? We had a gay conversation and I learned to
my amazement that she came from Longmeadow,

Massachusetts, my own home town. Her father was a well-known doctor in our community, her house only a couple of miles from where I lived.

My Dutch publisher entertained me that day. He was as gracious as my Danish one. In his car I had a chance to see a lot of Holland, driving to all the famous little places where the houses are below the water level and have little bridges leading to their doorways. Everybody clomped about in wooden shoes and in native costume, even tiny children dressed like the adults. I was most grateful to hear a little of the history of Holland and of its wonderful Queen and her family. It was a most memorable day, and I never regretted going there.

The next day I flew to London, which was even more magnificent then I had thought possible. It was Saturday and the publishing company office was closed, but one of the editors met me and I had tea with him and we had a chance to talk a bit. I stayed at a lovely small hotel and I went sight-seeing all by myself. I got along very well in England except for a mistake with a taxi. I was very confused about English money, so different from the other countries and especially America. The first time I took a taxi I didn't know what to pay the driver when he told me the fare. I filled my two hands with money and said to him:

"Please help yourself. I have no idea about English money."

He did! Later I discovered that that was the most expensive taxi ride I had ever had, and I blamed it on my own foolishness and a taxi driver's greediness.

After leaving England for Scotland where I spent only a few hours, seeing a little of its moors and millions of flowers, growing just anywhere, I returned to America.

It was a pleasant flight. I was pretty used to flying by that time, but best of all . . . we were flying home.

The sad part was I would have but a day with my family before I'd have to fly to Wisconsin where I was to speak at a Christian Writers' Conference.

It was hard to leave so soon. But I had promised and this was my new life; I must be grateful for the way I was received.

It was at that Conference I met the well-known author Margaret Lee Runbeck. How happy I am that we had time to talk and make friends. She was one of the dearest and sweetest Christians I had ever met. She invited me to visit her home in California . . . but only a month or so later God called her into the larger life. I know heaven is much richer with her there, but oh, how much we could have used her and more of her wonderful books here on earth.

When I was on the plane again for New York, this time home, to be really home for the summer, I relaxed for the first time in months. It seemed I hadn't stopped a moment since my book had come out the fall before. I was homesick, I discovered, because all the fame in the world cannot make up for the happiness of a home. I felt almost like a bride! My thoughts went back over the summer that was almost over, thanking God for the blessings I had received. I had never really felt alone though; God had been so close to me. And I repeated to myself again, to confirm my faith: WHERE I AM, GOD IS. With my hands in His I could go anywhere. His protection never failed. Life is such a sweet thing. How happy I was that I was born! Every day I must remember to thank God for life.

It was dark, so I could not see the land below me, but I knew how it looked from the plane. Little farms seemed like toy houses and roads like pencil marks and a tiny speck of blue was a lake. God bless America my dear homeland! The blessing that flowed from it had begun with the pilgrims who came here to have freedom to worship and pray. Their prayers were so great that they still hover over this country of ours. We are still living on those blessings they brought by their faith and love to their God and their new land. It is sad to know that among the good so much evil exists. But we must not be dismayed because the Master said, "This is what shall overcome the world—*our faith.*"

We must dare to walk with courage, knowing that each good thought will overcome one evil . . . our prayers for our Nation must never cease. We must believe in our America. We must choose a godly man to be our President and our love must begin in our own hearts and go out to our Home, our City, our State and our Nation. That is what God desires from us—that we love mercy, and do justly and walk humbly with our Lord. Perhaps the day soon will be here when our people will turn from wrong and walk the Pilgrim way . . . which also was the prayer way.

It was midnight as we flew in over New York City. Is there a more magnificent sight to see, than New York City at night from an airplane? Its miles and miles of lights look as though the whole firmament had fallen down to earth. We had had a little disturbance on this plane ride. There was a man who had become almost frantic as we flew over Lake Michigan. He had had a vision that we would crash in water, and he demanded life belts for all of us. When he was told there were none, he became very excited. The little sailorboy sitting beside me peered anxiously into my face.

"Do you think we will crash?" he asked, looking very tense and worried.

"Of course not," I smiled. "This is a good trip, God is with us."

"I think you are right," he said in a lighter tone. "I want to go home to my bride."

"And I to my husband. I have been away a long time. God is good to us; He will protect us."

As we landed, the disturber hurried off quickly. I wondered if he was angry that we hadn't crashed; he looked so disappointed.

The sailor shook my hand.

"Thank you," he said, almost as though I had been responsible for the safe trip, "I knew you were right. I can see you love God—it shines out from your eyes."

He hurried to the arms of his waiting bride. I looked for my husband. . . . I walked slowly. . . . Everybody seemed to be greeted by someone. . . . I was the last one through the gate. . . . He wasn't there!

I don't remember any other night like that. As the minutes ticked away on the big clock on the wall of the big waiting room, I told myself: He has been delayed. Very soon I will see him rushing toward me, explaining the reason he wasn't on time. Thinking that way made me calmer. I must remember something special . . . something gay . . . something funny. Memory is such a wonderful thing that God has given us. You can turn it back like the pages of a book. It was easy for me to think of an incident and so live it over again in my mind. It was one in the morning now and no sign of my loving husband, but I tried to face it bravely. . . . I would think of that time in greater Boston when I almost became the prey of a big, brusque police officer. I admit now that I was wrong, but the sign had said "Boston" and the pointing arrow had been as big as a billboard, and I had known that I had to follow that sign. I had come about one hundred miles from the New Hampshire way and I had another engagement; my time was short; I dreaded the heavy traffic, but I must make it on time. As I came to an intersection with three double lanes, I somehow got into the wrong one. Seeing the "Boston" sign, I knew I had to follow it despite the traffic, but I saw the policeman standing in the circle directing the cars. He was waving his arms this way and that, and to be sure he would understand my situation I opened my window and pointed to the left. He shook his head and pointed to the right. But I was *not* going to the right. . . . I didn't know where the right-hand lane would take me. . . . I had to go left . . . I had to go to Boston.

So, I didn't move. I just sat there. About fifty horns began to blow at me from all directions . . . the cop beckoned even more forcefully than before; his face was red as a beet, but I had still not made up my mind . . . I couldn't go right . . . I had to go to Boston. The policeman's lips were moving as though he was saying words under his breath . . . I knew I had to do something, so I suddenly shot over two lanes, straight to the left . . . to the sign saying Boston.

"Please dear God, glue him down," I prayed desperately. "I have to go this way."

But the Lord God did not hear my foolish prayer. A sharp whistle blew . . . the officer came towards me as I obediently pulled to the curb. I tried to be brave . . . I tried Mama's method. I smiled my prettiest.

"Do you know it is against the law to disobey an officer?" he barked.

"Officer, I did not disobey," I said meekly.

"Then tell me just what did you do? I motioned to you to go right, didn't I? But you just sit there, holding up a mile of traffic at the busiest time of the day . . . and when you finally decide to move you drive across two lanes of traffic and sail off to the left. . . . It is because of people like you that we policemen get gray hair before our time."

"Well," I ventured, feeling my way with every word. I was in trouble. Even God would not help me now. "I was going to Boston . . . and that sign as big as a house says Boston is that way. . . . I am to speak in Boston and I am late now. . . . I couldn't go the other way. I would not know where I was going. I have to follow signs. . . . I thought you would understand. . . . I couldn't talk to you . . . so I did what I knew I had to do."

"I understand perfectly, lady, and this little note will make you remember to obey the law. . . ."

I stared at him unbelievingly. "You are not going to give me a ticket!" I cried in horror.

"Well, what do you think I would be giving you?"

he snapped sarcastically. "Your license and registration, please."

I didn't move, but I looked pleadingly into his angry face, "I have never had a ticket and I have been driving eighteen years. You are not going to spoil it now, are you?"

He came closer and his voice was almost a whisper. "Do you see that officer standing at the corner. Well, he is the sergeant. If I didn't give you a ticket for the commotion you have caused, he would demote me. He saw the whole thing."

"Good," I said. "I am going over to talk to the sergeant."

"You are going to do what!" he almost screamed at me. "I'm warning you—the sergeant is a hard man."

I had reached the end of my rope. I was tired and I had never had a man talk to me in that tone of voice before. I felt the stinging tears coming into my eyes; there was no holding them back.

"I don't care," I sobbed. "I am going over and make that sergeant understand. I'll explain how I came a stranger into the town's worst traffic jam. I am confused and bewildered. I don't know where to go unless I follow signs . . . and you are not even nice to me. I'm not used to having men bark at me. . . . I'll never drive through this town again . . . and now you have made me cry and I am late for my appointment."

He looked confused for a moment. Then he began to wipe the sweat from his forehead. He looked sad and dejected.

"Lady," he said, looking past me. "I've never met a woman like you before. Please drive off . . . to BOSTON. As for the ticket . . . let's forget it—shall we?"

He walked quickly back to his post to direct his delayed traffic. I felt sorry for him. I was in the wrong . . . but apparently his bark was worse than his bite . . . and I—well, I had helped myself out of trouble . . . I still had a clear record . . . but I had used a woman's cheapest—and surest—weapon . . . *tears.*

Suddenly I realized I was still sitting on that hard bench in the airport . . . I was still waiting. . . . even reminiscing hadn't seemed to soothe my anxious heart. Where was my husband? Why didn't he come? It was one thirty-seven now! There must have been an accident . . . he would have called and had me paged otherwise. Perhaps he was hurt, lying on the road somewhere . . . perhaps he was in the hospital! He might even be dead. . . . But I mustn't let myself think such thoughts. I must have faith. Something might have happened at home that had delayed him. Why hadn't I thought of it before? I would call my daughter; she would know what time he left for the airport.

I got my daughter out of bed, but she was glad to hear my voice.

"I can't understand it," she exclaimed. "Dad left here at seven P.M. He wanted to be sure to be there when the plane came in."

As I walked back to my bench, my heart was in my toes. There must have been an accident he was involved in, but he would come . . . those things take time. I must be calm, I told myself. I would think of another funny incident, I would try to entertain myself. . . . The airport was almost empty now. Everybody seemed to have closed up their booths and gone home. There seemed to be no more planes coming in. I fought back the tears and made myself remember a certain time in a town in Pennsylvania. I had been speaking in the afternoon and had hours and hours to wait before the train would take me to Buffalo. To kill time I browsed around in a lovely gift shop. A lady I had met and struck up an acquaintance with accompanied me. She was good company and as always I was amazed at how wonderfully well things turned out for me. Suddenly she asked me a simple question.

"When did you say your train was leaving?"

"Eleven thirty, almost midnight," I answered.

"Are you sure?" she insisted. "There is only one

train going that way each night. If you missed it, you would not make your next engagement."

"I am sure! But I will look so we don't have to worry."

I opened my pocketbook and took out the ticket and looked . . . I looked again! I stared at it. Finally I gasped . . . it is leaving at eight fifty-five . . . and it is eight forty-five now. . . . What shall I do?"

"It takes twenty minutes in a taxi . . . and it takes time to get one, too. What in the world will you do?"

"Dial the station for me!" I cried, "I am too nervous."

She did the dialing and I got on the phone, gasping for breath in the small phone booth.

A pleasant voice answered, "This is the Union Station. What can I do for you?"

"Has the train come in?" I blurted out, trying to talk fast.

"It is just coming in now, lady."

"Please hold it for me. I will get a taxi right away. . . . I'll be there in twenty minutes . . . I have to get that train."

"Lady," came the astonished voice, "I can't hold a train . . . no one can hold a train for——"

"But you have to," I insisted, "I have paid for a sleeper on it . . . I have a speaking engagement . . . please. . . ."

"Listen," cried the voice on the other end, "the only one who can hold a train is the station master. I'll get him for you and you try to talk him into it. . . . Where did you say you were going?"

"I didn't . . . but I am going to Buffalo."

"Lady *that* train leaves at eleven fifty-five." The telephone clicked. She had hung up on me.

I just stood there; slowly I opened my purse again. I had looked at the wrong ticket . . . the one from Buffalo to home.

About eleven thirty that night I entered the Union Station in that little town. The clerk was just going off duty and her successor had come in. Just as she was leaving, she turned back and faced the other lady.

"I want to have you get a load of this," she said. "Of all the crazy women! You ought to hear the nutty one I had on the line tonight. She called up and demanded I hold that train. 'You've got to hold it,' she screamed at me. . . ."

As I stood there and listened, I heard my story getting bigger and bigger. Was she a good storyteller! Only she put in a lot of extra words that I knew I never had said. I couldn't help it then . . . I walked right up to the window.

"What can I do for you?" asked one of the ladies.

"Oh," said I, "I just wanted to introduce myself. I am that nutty lady!"

It perhaps wasn't very nice of me, but it was worth it to see the look on their faces . . . the situation had been bad enough the way it was without their adding to it. . . .

I looked at the time. It was almost two o'clock now. I couldn't think of any more stories. I was frantic with worry. I was so frantic I couldn't even pray. It looked as if my husband wasn't coming. Perhaps I would have to sit here all night. I took my suitcase and walked out into the air. There I sat down on the suitcase, close to the door. At least here I could see if he drove in. There wasn't a soul in sight. I had held my tears back so long that now I just let them roll down my cheeks. I had never felt so lost and completely alone. I heard footsteps and a nice-looking pilot walked by me. He took a look and stopped.

"Lady," he asked, "are you in trouble?"

"I sure am," I sobbed. "I have lost my husband. He was to meet me at the plane at twelve o'clock tonight and he never came."

"Well, that can happen," he said, smilingly. "You're not the first wife to be stood up."

"But you don't understand," I explained. "My husband is not like that . . . something has happened to him . . . he never would leave me like this. We love each other. He would die for me. I am so upset I can't even pray . . . if I could pray, all would be well."

"You are so upset you don't even know what you are saying," he said. "But let me ask you a very common question . . . one we very often ask in cases like yours. Are you sure you are at the right airport?"

"Of course I am," I answered sadly. "I am at the La Guardia Airport."

He looked at me. "No, lady," he said, "you are not. You are at the Newark Airport!"

Now I stared back at him.

"But how did I get here?" I asked bewildered. "The girl where I bought my ticket told me I would come in to La Guardia and I never looked."

He was just wonderful. He stuck by me and helped me get my husband paged at La Guardia Airport. The poor dear had been waiting there since eleven o'clock frantic with worry because I hadn't been on a plane that came in a half hour later than I had told him. . . . He had met every plane since. But when I suggested that he hurry over to pick me up, he told me in no uncertain terms I deserved to be left to take the train home in the morning. . . . Why in the world hadn't I found out where I was landing? But I know my man pretty well. I got him calmed down and when he picked me up at the Newark Airport and saw my red eyes, he forgot his anger and as we drove home those hundred and fifty miles to our own town and I sat there close beside him, almost forgetting that we had been married twenty-nine years, I felt as though I were eloping and we were off on our honeymoon . . . and I thank God that I can say we lived happily ever after.

Chapter Ten

As a child I often wrote letters to God as prayers. In the parsonage we children were taught to share everything with each other. If one was sad, it affected all of us. If something wonderful happened to make one especially glad, there was joy and laughter in the whole family circle. So I found sharing certain things easy, but I learned that when it comes to sharing those thoughts planted deep, deep down in our hearts, most of us would rather not. They are too sacred. They belong to us alone. Then I discovered that, by writing to God, I shared more of my inner life with Him than if I prayed in words. I still have many of those prayers, not from my early childhood, but from a later time in my life as a housewife, because even as an adult I often felt the need to talk to God the writing way. I never thought I would share these thoughts. I kept them in my desk where I could pick them up easily, and at times when my mind was very tired, I used to read them again as part of my worship for the day. I now want to share some of them with the world. Simple as they are, I want those who read them to remember they were not written as a lesson, or a story, but for me ... and me alone.

August 29, 19——
Dear God,
    This morning I started the first breath of awak-

ening with a prayer of praise. It seemed to set
the whole day right! I was almost walking on air
when I came into my kitchen to fix breakfast.
After we had had our devotion and my Bob had
left for his business, I hurried with my housework and when all was in order, I devoted twenty
minutes to being still. Father God, I have discovered that to be absolutely still in mind and soul
and body, to stop all thoughts and let every cell
in my body relax, makes it easy for me to hear
Your voice in my heart. I wait and let You talk
to me. It has taken me such a long time to be able
to be still twenty minutes. I used to begin with
five, and they really seemed so long. Now twenty
minutes does not seem any longer than five did.
I ended my silence by meditating on the Twenty-
third Psalm. All through the day I tried to catch
glimpses of You, in people's faces, in the birds
that sang in the trees in my garden, in the beautiful flowers and the golden sunset. But despite
all of that my day was not perfect. I didn't guard
it well enough. Negativeness crept in here and
there and many times I was impatient with those
around me. I am not happy about my progress
for today, but I will try to do better tomorrow.

Yes, these letters became a chart of my spiritual
life. I could check back and see how much I had
progressed in a certain space of time. It was almost
like a report card and I wanted to make high grades.
And I found that my writing did draw me closer to
God and closer to the best of me, although at times
I was very discouraged with myself.

September 1, 19——
Dear God,
    Today it seemed as though I failed in all I did!
My heart was heavy when I awoke because I carried yesterday's trouble with me into the new tomorrow. Instead of starting with a prayer, my
first thought was about myself. I felt tired and
distraught and my face showed it at breakfast-

time and made the rest of my family gloomy, too. I found the housework a heavy burden and grumbled about the many tasks that were awaiting me. Somehow I could not find a moment to have my quiet time. I was too busy. Now, as I look back over my day, I can see nothing in it of value for eternity . . . nothing to help the world. I am sorry because it could have been a good day if I had remembered that *prayer changes things*. I am resolved to do better if You give me another day.

September 22, 19——
Dear God,

Being a mother is such a wonderful thing! I marvel to think that You trusted me with two little daughters to mold and fashion in thoughts and deeds. I want so much to do my very, very best. I find it hard to be strict though, especially when two big blue eyes look up at me filled with glittering tears as I am about to administer punishment. When a small girl's voice sobbingly assures me that she is sorry and will never be naughty again, I sometimes can't go through with it. I hear myself saying, "Darling, Mother will give you another chance to be good!" I wipe her tears and her face lights up like a sun peeping through the clouds, and my heart is light once more. I hope she has learned her lesson and really and truly is sorry.

I can see myself as a child of Yours, saying the same words as I sin against Your holy will, and You always give me a second chance. Sometimes, though, You have to lay Your hand on me and I know then that is the best for me. I know it is Your love for me that makes You do it. I trust my little girls will know that when, in later life, they will look back on their childhood days. I don't want them to say I was a weak mother. I want them to know when I had to punish them my heart broke in little pieces, but I had to do the things that were necessary to help them grow up to be wise and strong and to walk with courage.

I will always remember how my own Mama told me that children are not our own, they are a precious loan from You. With such a loan we must try to be worthy of our little ones and bring out the very best in them to Your glory.

They both are sleeping in their little beds right now. A few minutes ago I went to their room and softly opened the door. I stood there a long time, my heart so full with joy I thought it would bust. I thought: Being a mother is the greatest thing in life . . . the highest calling . . . the finest profession. Because today's daughters will be tomorrow's mothers. They are the flowers that hold the seed for the new world without end. In a mother's heart you have planted so much of Your own goodness. Its love is deep enough and wide enough to last for a whole lifetime. A mother's love is really the only completely unselfish thing on earth. Even a husband and wife love to be loved back. A sister and a brother give back to us according to what we give to them. Our best friends expect a reward for their friendship and they are true as long as we are true to them. But the real mother asks nothing in return for her love. She prays that her little ones will grow up to be fine and good and true. There are mothers who sacrifice all the comfort of life to give their children an education, and there are other mothers who patiently and silently wait years for a prison gate to swing open so they can hold their crime-sick lost boy in their loving arms. Oh, Father God, just now that story my Papa used to tell in his sermons so long ago comes back to my memory. A story I never can forget and that truly pictures to us a mother's love.

He told of a prisoner who was going to be executed in a small town in a certain country far away. This town had an old tradition that a prisoner would hang when the bell rang from the town's only little church. The execution was about to start. All was set in order. The bell ringer had been told the time, but nothing seemed to happen. Some of the officials rushed to the

white stone church; they saw the bell ringer, pull-
ing the bell rope with all his might, but no sound
rang out. They sent a man up to the belfry to in-
vestigate and there they found the gray, wrinkled
little mother. Her hands were clutching the bell
clapper; they were bleeding and bruised but they
kept it from making the sound. Her heart would
not let the bell ring because that would signal
the death of her only boy. The legend tells that
the warden was so touched by this great mother
love that he stayed the execution and the boy's
sentence was commuted to life in prison. I have
always hoped that perhaps that boy was eventually given his freedom and became a good man
for his mother's sake, but the legend does not
say . . .

I am glad I was born a woman and that the
privilege of becoming a mother was given to me.
I have made up my mind always to try to live up
to its greatness. My heart almost breaks when I
read in the newspaper about mothers who have
lost their calling . . . who have fallen from
grace . . . oh, that they would wake up to the
fact that God's greatest gift was bestowed upon
them.

As I lift those letters now, one by one, and loving-
ly read them again, they stir my heart anew to serve
You better, God. I don't write letters to You any more.
That stopped when I became an author. Now I pray
more in words than I ever did before in all my life,
but there is an unwritten prayer in those words . . .
there is the same longing to love You more . . . to
serve You better . . . and I still try to keep those
silent moments. There is a terrific power in silence
. . . it surely is better than gold.

October 7, 19———
A wonderful new day! How thankful I am for
earth life. Each day I seem to know more and
have a better understanding of this journey. We
build here on earth for ourselves a house not

made by hands. We must live our lives so the world is better because of us. As our thoughts go out on the ether waves of time, they must carry strength and healing on their wings. I like to start each new day with this one thought—GOD —and I want to live each moment for one reason only—You, GOD, I want to end each day with my hand in Yours.

> Lift up your head and smile
> And living is worth while
> Be brave when days are dark
> With springtime comes the lark
> Be still and know . . . my soul
> That God has made thee whole. . . .

November 4, 19——
Dear God,
   My Bible verse for today is Psalm 3:3

> But Thou, O God, art a shield about me
> My Glory, and the lifter of my head.

What is a shield? An umbrella is a shield against the rain. A coat a shield against the cold. An apron a shield against the dirt. It is so precious to know that You, Lord God, are a shield for me against anything that could harm me. The greatest harm that could come to me would be those things that would crowd out the spirit of truth. Evil thoughts! My wonderful God, You have placed Yourself between them and me. You stand there as a bright, shining light and when I look at the light long enough, I can't see anything but the light. You are my guide! When I walk with You beside me, all is well within me. My soul rejoices in Your love. The little hurts of life that come my way I gladly endure because of my *Love for the Lord*, I say, "Because the mind of Christ dwelleth in me I want to bless and not curse . . . give, and not look for the reward." It is a big lesson to learn, this lesson of living a

triumphant life in this world. But I know I can
. . . and I will.

My girls are not little girls any more. They have
grown into adults and now should know how to walk
on the road of life. But how I remember the struggles
I had to try to give to them a strong foundation. I saw
them go into the mysterious, confusing years of adoles-
cence. I saw love come and love go in and out in those
tender years. I have seen them hurt when dark shadows had shut off the sun for a time, and I often cried
with them as they faced the storms of life. I told them
they must set their faces against the storm and walk
on to be made strong to meet the next one. I walked
miles and miles with them as we talked and they
opened the secretmost parts of their hearts and let me
look in. Sometimes one of them would say: "Mommie,
you understand better than any girl friend and I
know it is because you have lived through these
things . . . and, you know, you haven't forgotten."
And then there came times when I had to make a
choice to keep myself on the high pedestal where
they had placed me or to step down and let them see
me as I really was. There come great temptations to
our young people. Their emotional life is not stable
and sometimes young love runs away from common
sense. Once I talked this over with one of my daughters. She had told me how frightened she suddenly
had become of love . . . how it had failed her at a
time when she had believed it was life's highest and
most beautiful emotion. Her love had turned almost
into hatred for a young man she had believed was
only fine and good. I knew I must help her. It was my
duty to open her eyes so she would see and understand clearly that sometimes a frustrated emotion
is like a hurricane; it destroys in a few minutes what
has taken a lifetime to build up. But to do this I had
to share things buried deep, deep in my soul, things
I had thought I would never think of again because

they were not a part of my better self. That was the day I wrote only a short letter to God.

May 18, 19——

Sometimes it almost breaks my heart to have to bring up daughters. Why do dark shadows have to descend on young hearts so trusting and brave? Why does evil creep in like a snake to rob their garden of its flowers? Today You know I swung that heart-door of mine wide open as my daughter came to me hurt and bewildered because of the shape a beautiful love had suddenly turned into. Did I do right to tell her my story of the time the same thing happened to me? I hope so. Take my words and bless them that they may become a light . . . a beacon to lead her on . . . and, Father God, don't let her think less of me because of it.

Yes, I did tell her. It was spring! A big full moon peeked in on the porch where we were sitting lazily sipping our coffee. The air had something of expectancy in it, flowers were beginning to bloom and the leaves were still tender on the trees. As young love, I was thinking.

"I don't think I ever want to see him again," my daughter said with so much sadness in her voice my heart almost broke, too.

"Don't make hasty judgment, dear." I tried to make my voice light. "Love has to have its tests! If we love high enough, we try to understand and forgive."

Her mouth opened. "Mom," she cried, "you are taking his part! How can you?"

I patted her arm softly.

"Honey," I said, "I take his part because suddenly I am you. The years are rolling back. I am a young teenager and I have met with such sorrow my heart cannot take it . . . I want to hate, too, but after the young man told me his side of it, I knew what happened was my fault as much as his. Do you want me to tell you the story?"

"Yes, please do!" she said eagerly.

"I was often a very foolish little girl when I was young and sometimes my foolishness led me into awful situations. But, believe me, my dear, I wasn't bad. I just didn't know any better. I was in love . . . terribly in love! And I loved a boy of whom my parents did not approve. I saw him anyway, but only in secret. You see I didn't have the freedom that you have enjoyed. Your grandpapa was very, very strict. . . . I could go only with the boys from our church and they did not appeal to my fancy. One time when your grandparents had to go to a conference and stay overnight, I thought it was a golden opportunity. I was to stay at home and be in charge of my younger brothers and sisters and they went to bed early. So I invited my boy friend to come to the parsonage and spend the evening with me. Now, I didn't know it was wrong to invite a boy over to the house when I was alone there. No one had told me. After all I had four brothers . . . and—well, I thought nothing of it. The only wrong I thought I did was to be with a boy I was forbidden to associate with. I remember how I tried to make everything as romantic as I could. I had picked flowers for the parlor and there was soft lamplight and coffee and Mama's best cookies.

"He came late; the children were all asleep and it began as a wonderful evening, but in the late hours things went out of control. My knowledge about boys and life was very limited. I was naïve and innocent despite my progress in book-learning. My parents had never told me the dangers of love. I was almost scared to death! The night had been so enchanting until suddenly my young man stopped being a good-natured, gentle companion and turned into what I thought a real devil. And he, being frustrated and with young, uncontrolled blood pulsing through his veins had completely misunderstood my invitation. In those moments of terror I remember him flinging out the angry words at me: 'For goodness' sake, what did you expect? You invited me to spend the night with you, didn't you?'

"I knew, as always when I was wrong. But I had been brought up in a God-fearing home and what was right before God mattered a lot to me. I tried desperately to think what to do. . . . There was nothing but to pray to God in my heart . . . a sorry prayer, knowing how discouraged even God must be with me . . . just hoping He would help.

"'Please dear God,' my heart prayed, 'keep me from doing wrong. . . . I have learned my lesson. . . . I want to do the right thing. . . . I will even go out as a missionary to the heathen if you will help me tonight. . . . Oh, God . . . I am so frightened I am ready to die.'

"And the help came in a very strange way. I always marvel about the goodness of God to His erring children here on earth. The magnificence of it . . . the mercy . . . the patience. I became so calm inside it was as though I had had a cool shower; my mind was clear and my brain worked just at the time I needed it. 'Listen,' I said. 'You are so much stronger than I . . . I can't fight you any longer . . . but will you please let me tell you a story?'

"'A story,' he gasped, hardly believing he heard right.

"'Yes,' I said . . . 'you see the story is about you and me and it just came to me from nowhere. . . .'

"'Go ahead,' he said. 'I'll listen to your story.'

"I spoke softly at first, as though I was feeling my way through the darkness of my brain cells. Then my voice gained in volume and I spoke clearly and with confidence as I knew it was God's help to me:

"'It happened way off in America at the great Niagara Falls. She was a little tiny white lamb and she had gone off into the wilderness without the permisson of her parents . . . she had gone swimming in the lake above the big falls although she knew it was a very dangerous spot . . . the little lamb was young and foolish, you see, and she seemed to find pleasure in disobeying her parents. But as she was swimming in the cool lake, having a wonderful time, she saw a big black eagle circling in the sky. It spotted her and soon it had its claws in the lamb's thick wool, and together they were floating with the stream. That eagle had only one thought in mind: what a wonderful meal he would have on that tender lamb! But first he would play along with her making her think that he was only riding with her down the stream of the lake. 'As soon as we reach the edge of the fall,' he said to himself, 'I will lift her and we will fly off where I can share her as a fine meal for my family.' They came nearer and nearer the roaring waterfall and just as the eagle was about to lift her, he found the lamb too heavy . . . so he tried to fly off without her . . . but it was too late; his claws were buried so deep in the white fleece of his prey that he could not get them loose and a few minutes later they both fell over the fall and were crushed to pieces in the sharp stones below.'

"I stopped. . . . What a beautiful story that was! I was thinking. And it did speak to him and to me, too. It made a very deep impression on my young man. He was himself again and begged me to forgive him for the unpleasantness he had caused.

" 'But now,' he said, 'let me tell you my side . . . the viewpoint of a man. A girl should never play with a man's emotions to the extent that he loses himself. Remember that always, my dear. Don't judge a man for what he can't help . . . when a girl willingly places him in the way of temptation, it is her fault as much as his.'

"I always remembered that and I know it was my fault as much as his, that evening so long ago. But God heard my prayer and saved us both from going over the falls of temptation. . . . That is why I ask you

117

not to judge, before you examine your own heart before God."

She sat still a long time. Finally she looked up at me with tears in her eyes. Her arms went around me.

"Mommie," she said, "you are wonderful . . . but not just wonderful . . . I shall always, always feel I can tell you things because you are . . . you are human."

I know my story helped her and many other young people I had told it to . . . and it also teaches that God will help us in any situation when we honestly seek His help with all our heart.

In those years I often wrote little poems. Not for any other reason than that something seemed to sing within me and I had to put it down on paper. One summer I had had trouble with the youngsters in the neighborhood who wanted to play in my cool shady yard. My children were grown up then, and I felt as do so many other mothers, this was a time in life when I could enjoy stillness and peace, and I had a right to chase the children off. But one day a strange verse came out of my pencil, and I wrote it in my letters as I felt that it was a letter from God to me.

HIGH FENCES

They were too noisy, the children
   who came to play in my yard. . . .
My grass was too green,
   I had labored too hard
To let them invade to destroy
        and pull up
           and break down. . . .
I wanted the prettiest garden in town.

Because of this sin, I became quite
   restless . . . and more . . . I couldn't stand noise
my poor head was too sore
And so came a knock
on my fancy front door

And two big blue eyes looked up at my face,
While her little sundress was an awful disgrace.

"Can I play in your garden?" said she.
"I have Billy and Ginny and Ruthy with me. . . .
We can't play in ours. . . .
My Mommie is sick. . . .
And she says: 'You go on,
Or I'll take the stick. . . .' "

She smiled as she talked,
"You are pretty," she said.
"I like to play right by that
big flower bed."
And without an answer
They all ran to play.
And I stood there a moment
  as my fence tumbled down.
It might not be now . . . the prettiest place
This garden of mine . . . in life's mad race
But I am convinced . . . with my fences down
My yard is the happiest yard in our town.

Meditating in verse was so much fun! There was
no one to judge or criticize. God spoke to the heart
in many different ways. I wanted to fill my life with
Him, and I prayed that these little tryings of mine
would make lovely music in His ears, for He listens
to our faintest whisper when we love Him.

December 17, 19——
Dear God,
My will is Thine, my Lord.
Take it to Thy Heart
And warm it with Thy love.
It is a stubborn will
But a willing one. . . .
It is a strong will,
and it needs channeling
in the right directions.
I want it to do Thy will
completely . . . at all times

For time . . . and eternity . . .
So little I have to give . . .
But Father God, I want to live
My life just for Thee
So create in me
An honest sincerity. . . .

March 15, 19———
To be filled with God's love each day
Walk with Him every step of the way
To sing a new song
Of His love, all day long. . . .
To walk
And to talk
And to know
I am dear in His sight
He is here
As my heart . . . so near.

January 1, 19———
Dear God,

I know that what I do for others will come
back to me and either bless or curse. If I don't
pay my bills . . . I shall be lacking in my daily
living. If I use others just to get things out of
them, whatever I gain from it shall be lost in sickness or loss in other ways. How very clear the
Master's words come to me now: "As ye measure
to others . . . so it shall be measured unto you."

February 9, 19———
Dear God,

How wonderfully you have protected me and
in my devotion I have felt close to *You*. The other
day a thought came so vividly to my mind. God
has cut a pattern for my earth life and my celestial
garment in the world to come will be shaped from
it.

June 11, 19———
Dear God,

This is my wedding anniversary day! I love to
dream back. Life is surely like a story. This is our

story . . . our wonderfully, happy story. It is true, we have had our ups and downs. Sometimes I have been very provoked and at times my husband had a very trying way of sulking when I displeased him. But we have grown better with the years, through understanding and learning to bear and forbear. I have learned never to make hasty decisions. When I want to tell my loved ones off, I think: If I but wait until the morrow the waves of time will have washed the anger away and the cruel words will be lost in the sea of forgetfulness instead of being uttered. I have learned with the years to delay the evil words but never to wait with the good. I love being a housewife and having a lovely home to play in. I love each little nook and corner. Dear God, I can never thank You enough for the blessings of a home and the love of a family. If I had the years that I have lived as a wife back again, I would walk up the same church aisle and say the words, "I do," to the man I fell in love with . . . and who became my husband before God and man.

April 27, 19——
Dear God,

Last night something happened which was very hard to bear. One of my dearest friends tumbled down from the heaven where I had placed her, and she broke in little tiny pieces right before my eyes. I have to try now to put those pieces together again. It will take a long time and they will never look as beautiful as before, but if you who are the Master potter help me . . . perhaps ours will be a fine friendship again. We must learn to forgive and to forget. Friendship is too dear and rare to be broken. I am a very imperfect person, too. Sometimes one does things on the spur of the moment, and The Master said so long ago when His disciples asked Him how many times to forgive . . . not seven . . . but seventy times seventy. . . . I can't begin to count how many times You, God, have for-

Chapter Eleven

I am by nature a home-loving person. A home to me is not the structure of a house put together with all sorts of materials, or the color of the wallpaper or the size of the rooms. It does not matter how modest or expensive the furniture; that is not what makes the home. When I think back on all the different places my husband and I and our two daughters have lived in during thirty-two years of marriage, I know in my heart that each place we have called home is as dear to me as the other and I feel tenderness for all of them. Year by year we have added more to our home—a little more expensive furnishing and a lot more of ourselves.

The true feeling of a home can be tested by the way strangers react to it. It has always thrilled me when people who have been guests in our home have told me in kind words that they had found something special in our home life, something they could not place their finger on. I know the secret! And it is found not only in our home, but in all homes where God has been invited to make His abode. We have always wanted our home to be a sanctuary, where HE is the most important part and where a little bit of HIS love may rub off on those who enter in.

In Papa's and Mama's parsonage there was always a special time designated for the family to gather together for worship. As soon as we children were old enough to crawl about we became part of this circle, and soon we learned to kneel with the rest of the family. Before we understood the meaning of prayer we understood that we must be silent, and when we grew older, we learned that God existed in that silence and that kneeling was to worship Him.

When I married, my husband and I followed the family tradition of having a special time set aside for God. Soon this was as dear to us as the fellowship at home had been in yonder years, and our girls felt the same security in it as I had felt as a little girl. It became a pattern for our home life.

I stand amazed and bewildered when I hear of people who are great church workers and call themselves Christians, but neglect to pray as a family unit in their own homes. "People who pray together, stay together" and they become closer and closer to each other as the years go by. There is not one problem that prayer cannot solve.

When we have house guests, we make it a rule to include them in our prayer time. Sometimes they look a bit bewildered and I hasten to make clear to them that this is not compulsory, only an invitation to them to feel that they are part of our family circle. Never has a guest refused to take part and, after it is over, they have always expressed their gratitude for being invited to share with us such a sacred tryst.

It has been a joy to know that our daughters always thought of our fellowship with love and respect and it became such a natural proceeding to them that it never caused embarrassment. I used to wonder how they would react when they brought their friends home for weekends, after they left the home, for of course there was always a houseful of young people on vacation from college and special weekends. Having girls we gradually had more boy visitors on these occasions. And I used to make a little speech to them, saying that we always had fellowship and prayer after the evening meal, and inviting them to join us. They seemed to enjoy the prayer time, too, and said they looked forward to coming back and worshipping with us again.

Once there was a young man who had taken a fancy to our younger daughter and for the first time I hesitated about asking him to join us. He didn't seem like the type who would enjoy a prayer time. Nevertheless, I invited him as I had the others before. He looked a little surprised, but he was very sweet about it and said if this was our family routine he certainly would not want to upset it. We were happy to have him as one of us and I was ashamed afterwards to think how wrongly I had judged him.

The next time he came he told me he had been looking forward to our evening session and just as we were about to begin he said, "I have a great favor to ask of you. Would you let me conduct the family worship tonight? You see, I brought along a book my grandfather gave me years ago, I would like to read from it so we all could share its beauty."

Well, he conducted that worship as well as my Papa would have done. And though I knew he came because he took our daughter out, he surely loved this particular time we had set apart for God.

Since our family is grown up now and there are just my husband and myself at home, we have changed the fellowship period to the breakfast hour and find that time more convenient. Every morning we have a relaxed time together as we read from the Bible and some other appropriate special booklet on devotions and join in a prayer, the arms of which reach around our loved ones wherever they are. We mention them by name, one by one, asking a blessing over their lives, special protection for the day and help for us all to do God's will. And as we pray, we know that Mama is also taking all our names before God. She speaks each name sweetly and tenderly as she begins her new day. She has done this since the day we were born. Now there are fifty-one of us to pray for.

It is the prayer fellowship that gives our home that special warm something. It reaches out a joyous welcome to those who enter in, and also ties us as a family with the strongest cords on earth—the cords of love. It is the togetherness of a family that makes a home a true home.

One afternoon as I drove into my driveway there was a strange car waiting for me. I found someone sitting on our doorstep who eagerly came to meet me.

"I hope you don't mind me coming like this," she said, looking anxiously up at me. "I asked my minister to make an appointment with you for me, but he advised me just to drop in on you, assuring me you were the kind of person who wouldn't mind at all."

"He is right," I said. "I love people."

At first I thought she was a high-school girl until I saw the wedding ring on her finger. She had a sweet, open face with wide blue eyes that smiled before she spoke.

I invited her inside my home and after we were seated on the sofa in the living room she told me why she had come.

"I have been married only a few months," she told me. "I have read both your books and I have fallen in love with Mama and the way she made such a warm, happy home for her family—but that was years ago. This might seem silly of me to ask you, but I am looking for a recipe for a perfect home life. My husband and I want to have lots of children, too. I want so much to be a real special wife and mother. Since you wrote those books with such happy home life, I'm sure you are the one who can advise me."

"I think you are very sweet," I said. "And you are on the right track. I am sure you are going to be a perfect wife because you want to with your whole heart. I have no written recipe for a happy home life, but I know how one should be lived and I will try to share with you the secret of a happy home life even in these days."

"Oh, please do!" She smiled. "I promise you I'll try it out."

"To create a home," I began, "I believe is the calling and the destiny of a woman. God gave her all the ingredients for it, but it is the mixing of them that is important if the result is to come out successfully. You know, the home is the making of a nation. When the home fails, the nation fails."

"I know," she said, looking out through the window as if she were trying to span far into the years of tomorrow, "that is the trouble with our country today ... the home."

"It takes two to begin a family and the children to complete it, but the wife and the mother is the one who makes a home what it is. It can be a warm, dear place to live in, or just an empty shell where people spend their years together. As you have said, my Mama knew how to create a happy home. I learned the secret from her. She always said it is the little things, the small ingredients that are the most important. The wife is the first one up in the morning, having a tasty breakfast waiting for her family when they arise. A smiling face, a glad good morning, starts them out well on a new day. There is something special about a family sitting down together to begin their day with grace before they partake of food. As the children run off to school, they have a secure feeling in their hearts. They know, whatever the day may bring, this is the place they will return to, and whatever the world thinks of them, here are those who love and want them. If they have problems, they can sit down and talk them over together. Their mother makes it a point to be at home when they return from school ... she is glad to see them.

Her smile is their sunshine. Children from a happy home grow up in security and trust in life and their fellow men.

"And so with a man. If his home is right, it becomes his palace. He is King there! A man like that does not roam. He has all that he wishes for. During the day, his thoughts wander back to his dear family. It is for them that he works so hard and it is more then worth while. He remembers that morning he had that important engagement, how his wife made blueberry pancakes for breakfast because they are his favorite. He feels her embrace as he leaves in the morning and she is always at the window waving as he drives off . . . yes, he can see her many times during the day . . . standing there waving and smiling and her last words: "Have a good day, honey!" And the kids! Just good healthy kids, too full of life at times, but even though his head is tired and he longs for peace and quiet . . . it is wonderful to think of their arms around his neck . . . their wet, short little kisses. Junior will always see that the garage door is open for him at night. He blows the horn twice as he drives in . . . that's the signal to let the family know he is home. . . . How they chatter during dinner. Everyone trying to tell the happenings of the day. But Mom manages it. She tells them all to listen and take turns . . . she wants them to be more interested in the others' happenings than in their own."

"That is important, I can see that!" she exclaims. "I must remember that."

"Yes," I say. "To listen is a great art."

"And what else?" she asks eagerly.

"Oh, there are the usual things in every home. The TV programs the children love to see before bedtime, and also the story. It is good for Dad to read to the little ones; he gets closer to them that way. My husband used to boast that there wasn't a fairy tale he didn't know. He always did the reading to the girls when they were small. And then one must see that the children kneel to say their prayers; sometimes they need a little help. A few moments to talk before they are tucked in and the tender good-night kiss: 'See you in the morning! Sweet dreams!"

"The house is still now as the husband and wife sit down in their easy chairs. The husband loses himself in his newspaper and the wife thinks back over the day. It is like the pages of a book. This a true story! The family lives a story each day. She is satisfied because she has tried her best, and tomorrow she will try even harder. The happiness of her family is her whole world.

"The weekends are so important. The chores they do together, each one taking a special interest in anything that has to do with *home*. There might be a game to see on a Saturday afternoon and at night a good movie to which they all can go together. The parents realize how fast the years go by and that soon the children will be grown up and the things they do now will be the memories they will have from their childhood days.

"I like to think of Sunday as the day that crowns them all. The husband cooking breakfast and having it ready when the rest of them wake up. This is his wife's morning off. They come up to his call blurry-eyed and stretching; they scramble to the table in nighties and pajamas and the wife says what she says every Sunday morning: 'No one can cook bacon and eggs like Daddy. Please, honey, don't ever change the Sunday-breakfast menu.'"

"There is something dear about a family going to church together, dressed in their best as they drive off in the family car. The day has begun right and it will be a day of perfect fellowship . . . and——"

I stopped suddenly.

"It was a long recipe," I said, "I'd better stop now. A recipe can be too long, you know."

"Thank you," she whispered, making ready to leave. "Someday write it in a book, will you?" She clasped my hand. "I am so glad I came. I am richer now and I feel I know so much."

I waved at her from the doorway. What a wonderful little person she was! I was thinking. So young and eager to build the right kind of home. There must be many more like her. If only all brides would begin like that, searching for the key to happiness . . . true happiness, how rich our world would be!

Chapter Twelve

Having grandchildren is a God-given blessing that lifts us out of the hum-drum of life and fills us with joy and fun. How wise God was to know that we needed that special gift when our years perhaps might seem duller and our pace begin to slow down a little. . . . In our children's children, we live our lives all over again. It is a different joy, though; we can share the fun without having to carry the burdens. When we get tired of their noise, we retire to our own haven of rest, so grandchildren are really ours to enjoy.

But to be a new, first-time grandmother is something else again! Thinking back now, I wish there could be a school for brand-new grannies where they could learn the first step of how not to interfere. I was not a very wise grandmother to begin with, but I learned . . . and learned the hard way. If I only had known at the start what I know now. If I had stopped to think, but most of all if I had prayed about it and let God guide my steps . . . but I didn't. This great gift I almost took for granted because it just seemed to happen to me. It is very difficult to learn that grandchildren first of all belong to their own parents. That they are ours to love and hold in our arms and lavish our affection and money on . . . but when it comes to giving advice . . . beware! We, according to our offspring, strange as it might seem, belong to a past generation. They feel things are different now. Life is a big crazy circle, for hadn't I felt the same way when I thought my parents came from the old dark ages?

Now I can smile as I think of my foolishness and forgive today's younger generation; I can do it now that I have learned. Any educated grandmother must know that you wait until you are asked for advice and that you willingly and gladly stay on the outside of the new circle of mystic fellowship until you are suddenly ushered into it.

There is a beginning to every story. Let me share mine, as, with great pleasure, I wander back and try to recapture the feeling I had when it began. This story belongs to a very young father and a still younger mother and a little redheaded chubby baby boy. Perhaps it all would not have been so complicated if our young people had not lived in our home when the great event took place.

They had met and married in college. Our daughter had just completed her first year, and her husband his third. I remember how I had dreaded that day when we would drive her out to St. Paul, Minnesota, where she was going to be enrolled in the college of her choice. It was a Swedish college, the same that so many of my sisters and brothers had attended and I had been happy and proud that she had chosen her family's old Alma Mater. What an empty household ours had been without our older daughter and how we missed her! She had been the lively, bubbling-over one, the one who couldn't wait to come rushing home from school to tell me in detail all the things that were going on. No more came the gay music from the piano she played so well and her songs that used to fill every room in the house. Her bed stood untouched and made up and my heart suffered untold agony. How soon they grew up. But this was part of life. A great adjustment that had to be made. And I was not alone in my grieving; there were millions of mothers who just now suffered the same way, and bore it bravely because this, too, was part of motherhood. But I counted the days and marked each one off with a pencil on the calendar as I waited for December and Christmas when we would see her again.

And Christmas finally came. A lovely white Christmas with evergreens and tinsel and lights and decorations shining everywhere. She came home, but not alone. Of course we had been told beforehand that a new young man would accompany her home . . . and more, much more than that . . . the newspapers on Christmas day would carry her picture with the announcement of their engagement. But when we were told they wanted a wedding the coming June, we put our foot down. Why, she was only a girl, too young to know her own mind, and we had hoped so much that she would get her education first before she began to think of marriage. But it was to no avail. Their minds were made up. All their classmates, almost, were getting married and they were to live in that cute apartment for married students on the campus. Girls did marry young nowadays and we seemed to be the only parents in the world who did not understand. I still worried about it. There had been a long high-school romance and it had seemed as if those two had been made for each other. College had changed all that! But would this love last? Did the young man know how headstrong this lovely daughter of ours could be? Would he know how she needed lots and lots of tenderness and understanding? It was so important for a marriage to be right and I felt they were too young to know, but all my talking did not even make an impression, so we gave up and I threw myself into planning the most beautiful wedding a girl could ever have.

And it was a lovely, lovely wedding. They looked so happy and everything began to seem more right. When they returned after a short honeymoon to pack their things and go back to their college town, my heart did not ache as much as the first time.

"This is life!" I told myself. Our girl had a right to

plan her own life. All I could do was to pray for her happiness.

They returned to college and I settled down to housecleaning and planning of winter clothes. Then, one sunny fall afternoon, I heard a car come into our driveway. Wondering what company was arriving, I looked through the dining-room curtain, only to run quickly to the front door and open it wide, for there they were, the two of them, in their old car, waving and smiling as though they had inherited the world. It took me a while to come to my senses, but suddenly my mind was clear. What in the world were they doing home with the college fifteen hundred miles away? . . . There was no vacation now . . . they both should be in college. They saw the anxious look on my face and after our greeting my daughter told me excitedly with stars dancing in her eyes:

"Mommie, prepare yourself for a shock . . . we are home! Home to stay for good. We have both quit college!"

"You have what?" I finally managed to get out in a faint whisper, praying in my heart I had heard wrong.

"Come, let's sit down together," said my daughter, "and while my husband unpacks, you and I can talk."

We sat close together. I was trembling inside. What in the world could have happened? Had they been expelled?

"Mommie," said a small voice, so like the little girl who used to be. "I have something very important to tell you, so important that you will gladly forgive us for quitting college."

I tried to listen . . . to shut off my thoughts, to be calm, come what may, but my heart was beating like a sledgehammer and I was sure it could be heard at the end of the street.

She held my hand, and she was so very young. Her golden blonde hair curled softly around her cheeks. Her eyes so wide and blue held a mysterious light, as though two stars had lost their way and found a place in there.

"Mommie," came her voice again. "Mommie, do you know what? You are going to have a grandchild!"

My heart almost stopped. The news had come so unexpectedly. So utterly unexpectedly. Of course I had hoped that someday this would happen, but I had thought they would at least finish their education first, and have a home of their own, and my son-in-law would have a position which would enable him to support a family . . . but this . . . right now . . . two crazy kids with nothing but themselves to start with. And my little girl, only one year of college . . . and her husband only one year left and now he had thrown it over . . . just like that. I couldn't even smile. My heart was too filled with worry.

"But I thought you would graduate first," I blurted out. "I thought both of you would realize this is really not the time . . ." I stopped. My daughter's eyes began to fill with tears and she gave me a look of contempt as she left the room and rushed out to throw herself into the arms of a loving, understanding husband.

I sat in the same place for a long time. Regret filled my soul. What a fool I had been! How tenderly and sweetly she had told me, acting as though she was giving me the biggest gift in the world. And I had pushed it away. I had refused to accept it! I had no words of happiness, just an accusation, and now she had left me and something between us had been broken that would take a long, long time to mend.

It took a little while for her to give me her confidence again, but after we all had had a talk and my husband in his calm way had made me try to see things through the youngster's eyes, the old warm relationship was restored. After all, he had said, a little bride of eighteen can't help losing her balance when she knows she is going to bring forth a new little life.

Of course she wanted to come home to be with us. And a husband, very much in love couldn't think of having fifteen hundred miles between them, so he thought quitting was the only logical thing to do. They would have a whole lifetime to catch up on their education, but to have their very first baby—well that was more important than anything else in the world.

Life became calm once more. Calm and busy. We did a lot of baby-clothes shopping and we planned and talked and dreamed. Sometimes I almost wondered if it was I or my daughter who was having the baby, the way it affected my whole life. It was wonderful to touch little booties and to put soft woolly little sweaters to my cheek and to count the dozens and dozens of diapers. And there was a brand-new crib and a bassinet and all those tiny little ingredients that make up that heap of things it takes to welcome the first baby. Evenings we sat and talked in front of the open fire and I used to relate little things from the time my girls were babies. Where had the years gone to? Could it really be true that soon now I would hold a little grandchild in my arms?

As time went on we had to face facts. Our house was too small with so many in it and with the baby coming. If they were to stay with us, we had to sell our little dreamhouse and buy a bigger place. It was a sacrifice to sell it. There were so many sweet memories connected with this place where we had lived so long. But we found a fine home with two bathrooms and we moved and settled down in new surroundings in plenty of time before the great event. My husband and I gave up the big sunny master bedroom so the baby could have more sun and light and time sped by and so the day arrived.

I had everything in order. There was a private nurse waiting in the hospital when my daughter arrived there. I had had three babies without a private nurse, but something could go wrong and I wanted to take every precaution. She had no idea what it was to be in labor. And there were those long, long hours in pain and waiting. The nurse helped *me*, more than my daughter. Just knowing she was there made me feel better. When the phone rang and my son-in-law joyfully told me of the little boy, I was wild with happiness. And so that night my husband and I climbed the stairs of the hospital and stood in front of the big window to get the first glimpse of this miracle child. He was so tiny and so sweet and so redheaded, it left a warm soft glow in our grandparent-hearts. Our first grandson! He was real! I was too happy to sleep that first night. Already I was busy making plans for his future . . . for his vacations home with us and, of course, for his home-coming.

The day arrived! A beautiful sunshiny June day. The roses were blooming and I picked a big bouquet to make the house look festive. After my son-in-law had driven to the hospital to bring his wife and baby home, I sat down by the window so I could look up the street, while I waited I hummed the old lullabies. Perhaps I could sing him to sleep nights. I wanted this little boy to feel the warm welcome that awaited him in his grandparents' house. If only that car would come. I hoped my son-in-law would drive carefully. The baby was too small to be shaken up. Suddenly I saw the car! I took one last glance at the house. The crib was ready with handmade sheets and soft blankets and a big Teddy bear in one corner. When the car stopped, I was waiting on the sidewalk. I was all ready to take him in my arms for, of course, I would carry him in. I greeted my daughter with a hug and a kiss and whispered, "Put that little bundle of joy in my arms. I want him to feel so welcome!"

But my daughter just stared at me in unbelief.

"Mommie, you're not going to carry the baby. Not this time. This is our very first baby and its Mama shall carry him in."

"But, darling," I insisted, "you are not strong enough yet! You shouldn't carry anything for many weeks."

"But I will carry my baby. I wouldn't miss it for the world. And, Mommie, I want to say this kindly, we sort of wanted to make believe we had our own home . . . would you . . . could you . . . please don't mind it, Mommie dear . . . but could we be alone with him just for the first hour?"

I was in the kitchen of my house so quick they never had time to see the hurt in my face. I heard a car door slam. They came up the walk and went slowly, slowly up the stairs. They were cooing and talking and I knew they were looking their son over, counting his fingers and toes. There was hugging and kissing and more baby-talk. It was a joyful fellowship upstairs in the intimate family circle and I, the grandmother, stood alone in the kitchen with tears streaming down my cheeks. My own daughter! How could she do this to me? I was so filled with self-pity I had no joy in my heart at all for their complete happiness in each other. All I could think of was how I had planned and dreamed and waited for this moment. And we had given up the best room in the house for them. We had sold our dear little home that we had loved so much . . . all we could think of for their happiness we had done, and what did they give us back . . . disappointment and heartache . . . that's all. "Please, Mom, leave us alone . . . we want to be just us . . . our little family." The hurt was so big I thought I was going to die.

Finally they called me. I could come up now and see him, but I'd better have a hanky over my mouth . . . and don't go too near the crib.

Well wasn't that noble of them, I fumed inside and, feeling very old and tired, I mounted the stairs. I looked, but my heart wasn't in it. I spoke in a strange voice. "Isn't he a lovely big baby!" the voice said, but there was no music in it.

"When he gets older, you can hold him," my daughter promised generously. They didn't notice my ex-

138

pression or my red eyes. They hardly knew I was there. They were giving the baby its supper.

It was much later after I had cried in my husband's strong arms that it came to me how selfish and silly I had acted and the only thing that was hurt was my pride.

"I know it hurts, dear," my husband had said ever so gently, "but don't take it so hard; they are so young and so wrapped up in their happiness they have room for nothing else. Wait, and someday they will come to you. They will beg you to be part of them. Here, give me a big smile now."

But I couldn't smile. I couldn't smile for weeks. They didn't need my advice . . . they had a babybook and if something went the least bit out of order they called their doctor.

But those awful weeks passed by somehow. I tried not to intrude . . . to remember my place. And then one night the baby had a long crying spell. They couldn't find anything in the book on how to stop it. They called the doctor. He advised them to let the baby cry until he stopped. They held him and walked with him . . . and still the cry became louder and louder. Then it happened. . . .

"Mommie," called my daughter from their room, "can you tell us what to do? Can you stop him?"

I flew into the room. "Please, God, don't let me fail," I prayed.

Gently I picked up the little bundle from the crib. I put my cool hand on his hot little face, I cuddled him close, so very close to my heart, letting all the love that dwelt there surround him. I sat in a chair and rocked slowly back and forth while a sweet old lullaby came from my lips. He stopped crying and soon he slept peacefully in my arms.

The young parents just stared at me in unbelief.

"Why, Mommie," cried my daughter, "how did you do it? Would you want us to move the crib into your room if he starts in again? Mommie, you are a wonder!

Why didn't we know you would know about babies better than both books and doctors. We should have come to you first."

That was my graduation from the school of grandmother—school of self-discipline. I had received my diploma as fast as that. I watched him that night. The minute he stirred I was beside him. I was delirious with happiness. I really, really had a grandchild.

After that night all the strict rules for the grandmother were erased. I had a chance to spoil him a little before they moved into their own home. When the second baby was due, I was trusted to come in and take care of the first one. He was a big boy by that time. I was very careful now because I knew how to act with a new grand-baby. It was just to remember . . . not to look . . . not to touch . . . not to advise and not to interfere. I didn't even go down to the sidewalk this time when they came home, and I was as happy as a lark. After all the boys were their babies . . . I had had mine. I could even understand now how important it had been for them to establish themselves that first time. I really had learned! Babies belonged to grandmothers just a little bit . . . and mostly when they cried. But as I waited for the young parents to come up the stairs with this new baby . . . my son-in-law came running up alone.

"We thought perhaps you would like to carry him up," he said, a littly shyly.

If I wanted to! . . . Never had a prouder grandmother carried a little dark-haired baby boy up a flight of stairs . . . I carried him into his room and put him down in the crib and I was personally there to help count all his fingers and toes. A grandmother's heart! What a strange contraption! And I was amazed to know how soon she could forget a hurt . . . if she only put her mind to it. Because I really felt as though that first time had never been and I had been in that mystic circle from the very beginning.

I have four little darlings now. Three boys and a

sweet little girl . . . and the way they hug and kiss and love me . . . all my grandmother's pains are over. Now I just share all their joys.

If only there were a school for new grandmothers-to-be many others would not have to learn the way I did. But being a grandmother is a most wonderful thing . . . and different from all other joys . . . and there will never be a dull moment with all those new little lives to dream and plan for.

Chapter Thirteen

As I consider our world today, I can't help but think how much young mothers could help their children build a firm foundation of faith in God if they would but practice telling them stories of the great men of the Bible. A story does something to a child's mind. It paints a picture which will be a companion in times of stress and loneliness.

As I reminisce now, I find that some of the gold nuggets from my childhood were the Bible stories Mama told me before I was old enough to read. I can hear her sweet voice still bubbling over with excitement as it placed in my mind pictures of the great men of the Bible. Let me tell you Mama's version of Enoch, the man that walked with God.

"You see," said Mama, "it happened this way: Enoch and God were very close friends, so close that every night they went walking together. One night they walked very far, because they had so much to talk about that they walked almost into the star-studded sky. And when they stopped to say good night, God held Enoch's hand for a long time smiling a wide and happy smile.

" 'We have walked so far tonight,' he said. 'We are a lot nearer my home than yours. Why don't you come home with me tonight?'

"Enoch thought that this was a very good idea, so he walked along with God into the golden streets of

Heaven. When he awoke the next morning and saw the beauty of God's world, he liked it so much that he never returned to earth."

What a picture of eternity that was to a little girl's mind, especially to one with a vivid imagination. Oh, I used to think so often, as I looked up at the sky, how beautiful it must be behind those clouds and how lucky Enoch was that God had invited him home to spend a night.

Another dear tale was the story of Isaac.

"It was such a terrible thing," Mama said, "and very, very hard to understand. God told Abraham to take his son, whom he loved just as much as any daddy could love his little boy, and offer him as a sacrifice on an altar far off on a mountain. Abraham obeyed, for he loved God even more than he loved his son or anything else on earth, and although it almost broke his heart, he took the things he would need and told his little Isaac that they were going for a long walk. So little Isaac kissed his mama good-bye and off they went. It was a nice sunny day with the birds singing and Isaac was singing, too. He thought it was fun going for a walk with his daddy and he ran along ahead, picking up sticks and stones, throwing the stones away but saving the sticks in case his daddy would need them to put on the altar. When they came nearer to the place, Isaac began to wonder a little. Always before, when they had gone to build an altar to offer a sacrifice to the Lord, they had had the sacrifice trotting along behind them. But now they had everything but the sacrifice. He asked his daddy about it, but Abraham only smiled a sad little smile and patted Isaac's curly black head and said almost as softly as a whisper, 'Little son, God will see that we have a sacrifice for our offering.' So Isaac took his daddy's hand and they walked the rest of the way together. When they had built the altar, Abraham lifted little Isaac up and placed him on top of it.

"'Now,' he said, 'we will play a game. I shall tie

you on this altar as if you were to be the sacrifice.' Although Isaac was a little frightened, he laughed because he saw the love in his daddy's eyes and said, 'This is a funny game, Daddy. I feel almost as though I was going to be offered.'

"Abraham had concealed the long knife behind his back, not knowing just how he could thrust it into his laughing little boy. Finally, when he thought he had gathered up enough courage to do it, a shining angel stood behind him and took the knife from his hand.

"'Don't touch that little boy,' the angel whispered in his ear. 'God was only testing you. He wanted to see how much you were willing to offer up for Him. You see, Abraham, you are going to be a great man and people shall know about you through all the years to come. Go out tonight and count the stars, and know that the same number of people shall come from you. And the Lord God says that He shall bless you always, and your people after you.'

"And right then and there Isaac saw a big goat caught in a bramble bush. 'Look Daddy!' Isaac cried. 'I see the sacrifice God has found for us.'

"They offered the sacrifice and praised the Lord, and then hurried home so quickly that they almost ran because they were both so happy."

I remember Mama saying to me as she looked deeply into my eyes, "You will never know what God will ask of you, my little one. But always obey Him, because He loves you more than you can ever love Him. No matter how bad things may look to you, He will never let you get hurt."

One of my very favorite stories was that of Daniel in the Lions' Den. Mama had to tell it over and over again and my heart always pounded when she told it, even though I knew the outcome.

"And they threw Daniel down into a pit of lions that were very, very hungry. They were so hungry that they could almost have eaten each other. Daniel landed on his face and when he sat up, the lions all

came rushing at him as though they were trying to
see who could reach him first. But Daniel wasn't a
bit afraid. He knew that God had told him never to
worry because He would always look after him and
as he was thinking of God, he began to shine. There
he sat, in a big shining ring of fire and all the animals
stopped dead! They were sore afraid. Daniel sat
there shining the whole night through and in the
morning, looking up, he saw the King at the top of the
pit and heard him calling his name in a very anxious
voice. 'Daniel, Daniel! I am very glad to see that you
are not hurt. You have proven to me that your God is
a God of might.' As Daniel was brought up from the
pit, the King wanted to know more about his God."

That story really helped me when I was afraid.
Didn't God protect Daniel? Then he would take care
of me. . . . Mama had told me so many times.

But my favorite of all favorites was the story of
David. As a child, I had had Mama tell me often about
the little shepherd boy who was so brave that he had
killed a giant with a little flat stone. I never tired of
listening to all the stories she told about David. As I
grew up, I read about his life over and over again.
This was the man whom God loved in a special way,
even though David was far from perfect. He sinned
in many ways, but God always forgave him. That ap-
pealed to me because I, too, had sinned often and
God had forgiven me. David even fell in love with a
married woman, taking her husband from her by
placing him in the fiercest battle where he was killed.
But, oh, how sorry David was, even though he was a
King, when he realized what he had done. God pun-
ished David and the whole kingdom even though he
loved him. Sin did not pay—it never had and never
would. David again received forgiveness and tried to
please God. David loved God so much that he wrote
many, many beautiful psalms to God's honor and
glory.

As I travel on the highways to speak in near and

distant places, I have much time to think. Sometimes the ride is very long and I am apt to be impatient. At a time like this, I keep my mind on God. I have read and committed many Psalms to memory. At stop lights and in traffic I often pray the Lord's Prayer—it takes *one* Lord's Prayer for a red light. This keeps my mind refreshed and my heart is lightened.

Often I meditate on the Shepherd's Psalm. One special day as I was driving alone to an engagement two hundred miles away, I felt King David very near. I let my imagination run away with me and I had the King ride along with me. We had a wonderful conversation. I told him that, of all his Psalms, I loved the Shepherd Psalm best.

"Now, King David," I said aloud there in the car, "I hope that you don't mind if I add a little of my own version to your wonderful Twenty-third Psalm. You see, I am a writer, too, and we could sort of have this Psalm together."

And I made believe that King David told me to go right ahead, and I wrote my own words between the lines of the Psalm.

As I close this book, that has been such a joy to write, I want to share with you just what I added to the Shepherd Psalm that special day, and later wrote down on paper.

THE LORD IS MY SHEPHERD
I SHALL NOT WANT
  I shall not want anything but my Shepherd.
    He is strong
      and wise
        and wonderful
And He loves me although He knows my faults,
And even the sin and selfishness that beset me.
    He loves me for what I am,
     And when I am tired and weary
HE MAKETH ME TO LIE DOWN IN GREEN PASTURES
  In the lush soft grass, I rest
  And He stands guard over my thoughts

So no disturbing ones enter in.
I let go of my burdens and cares.
I am still and know that He is God.
When I am rested and refreshed, ready to start
 my earth's journey, again

HE LEADETH ME BESIDE THE STILL WATERS.
 I sit there in the quiet of the evening
 And see the sun sink behind the mountains.
  In that golden hour
  my heart finds peace,
 My striving ceases and I surrender to His will
  and now

HE RESTORETH MY SOUL.
 Yes, he takes my hand and holds it fast
  While we walk past the many forks in the road.
 How easily I could have chosen the wrong one
   Had he not been with me
       but,

HE LEADETH ME IN THE PATHS OF RIGHTEOUSNESS
FOR HIS NAME'S SAKE
 It is a narrow path . . . but oh, so beautiful!
  The birds sing in the early morning
  While the grass is wet with dew;
  The sun shines and the air is fresh and pure.
 If I let go of my Shepherd's hand and wander off
   and get lost in the deep forest
    of wilderness,

YEA, THOUGH I WALK THROUGH THE VALLEY OF THE
SHADOW OF DEATH I WILL FEAR NO EVIL.
 He will seek me until He finds me
 And when I grow weary and faint and falter
    because fear chokes me
     and my vision fails me
 As the shadows grow deeper and darker—then I
      remember.

FOR THOU ART WITH ME
THY ROD AND THY STAFF THEY COMFORT ME.
 They protect me from all ills.
THOU PREPAREST A TABLE BEFORE ME IN THE
PRESENCE OF MINE ENEMIES
 Whose names are: Fear, Worry, Selfishness and
 Insecurity.

When they see me drink of gladness and joy
and eat of perfect peace,
They leave me,
And then
THOU ANOINTEST MY HEAD WITH OIL.
The gentleness of His hands almost makes my
heart
burst asunder with happiness
yes, oh yes.

MY CUP RUNNETH OVER
It is too full. . . . I have room for no more
There is no limit to the abundance of gifts
which the good Shepherd bestoweth on me.
His gifts are from the best of the land.
So I shall never be lonely
He gives me companions.

SURELY GOODNESS AND MERCY
SHALL FOLLOW ME ALL THE DAYS OF MY LIFE
and as we walk along together
one day . . . at dusk . . .
I shall come to a bend in the road,
I shall stop,
and far off in the distance I shall see a
Mansion.
It is magnificent in its glory
It is a House not made by hands,
eternal in the heavens
And only the single eye of the soul
can behold it.
I shall bow down and worship
and as I walk silently
toward it
My heart leaps with gladness . . .
A thousand stars spring into space
All the song-birds on earth sing
and the little children laugh
And their laughter echoes back
through God's heaven
into the angelic chorus of the saints.
I have forgotten my yesterdays
and all the many tomorrows
because I shall enter . . .

AND I WILL DWELL IN THE HOUSE OF THE LORD
FOR EVER
... AND EVER ... AND EVER ... AMEN!

ABOUT THE AUTHOR

THYRA FERRÉ BJORN was one of eight children born to a clergyman and his wife in Swedish Lapland. She came to America with her family in 1924, when her father was called by a Swedish church in Springfield, Massachusetts. It is this parsonage background that has enriched Mrs. Bjorn's bestselling books, including *Papa's Wife, Papa's Daughter, Mama's Way, Dear Papa, This Is My Life, Once Upon a Christmas Time* and *The Home Has a Heart*. Thyra Ferré Bjorn has two daughters and six grandchildren, and she and her husband make their home in Longmeadow, Massachusetts. Through her frequent lecture tours she has become well known throughout the United States.

Bantam Book Catalog

Here's your up-to-the-minute listing of over 1,400 titles by your favorite authors.

This illustrated, large format catalog gives a description of each title. For your convenience, it is divided into categories in fiction and non-fiction——gothics, science fiction, westerns, mysteries, cookbooks, mysticism and occult, biographies, history, family living, health, psychology, art.

So don't delay——take advantage of this special opportunity to increase your reading pleasure.

Just send us your name and address and 50¢ (to help defray postage and handling costs).